BEAUTIFUL STAR OF BETHLEHEM

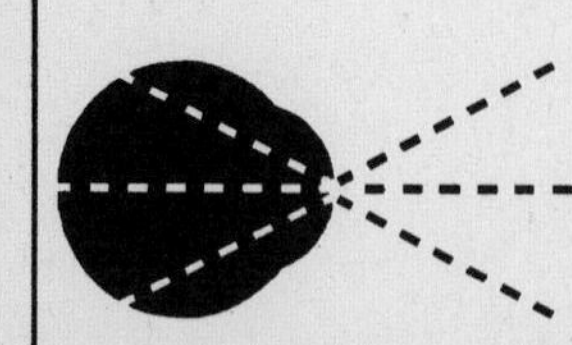

This Large Print Book carries the Seal of Approval of N.A.V.H.

Beautiful Star of Bethlehem

Lori Copeland

THORNDIKE PRESS
A part of Gale, Cengage Learning

GALE
CENGAGE Learning

Farmington Hills, Mich • San Francisco • New York • Waterville, Maine
Meriden, Conn • Mason, Ohio • Chicago

Thorndike Press, a part of Gale, Cengage Learning.

Thorndike Press® Large Print Christian Fiction.
The text of this Large Print edition is unabridged.
Other aspects of the book may vary from the original edition.
Set in 19 pt. Plantin.

LIBRARY OF CONGRESS CATALOGING-IN-PUBLICATION DATA

Copeland, Lori.
Beautiful star of Bethlehem / by Lori Copeland. — Large print edition.
pages cm. — (Thorndike Press large print Christian fiction)
ISBN 978-1-4104-8445-1 (hardcover) — ISBN 1-4104-8445-9 (hardcover)
1. Large type books. I. Title.
PS3553.O6336B43 2015
813'.54—dc23 2015032843

Published in 2015 by arrangement with Barbour Publishing, Inc.

Printed in Mexico
1 2 3 4 5 6 7 19 18 17 16 15

To my granddaughter,
Ella Parker Copeland,
born December 27, 2011.
Your "Poppa" and I adore you,
Miss Ella.

Chapter One

December 1, 2014, 7:12 p.m.

Burlington, Vermont

I forgot my pantyhose.

The thought hits me when our car pulls through the private terminal airport gate ablaze with Christmas lights. I knew I'd forgotten something.

After thirty-two years of marriage, Jack and I are finally grandparents of a beautiful baby girl weighing in at five pounds two ounces, and I packed a dress and forgot to throw in pantyhose.

In a little over three hours, I will be holding my darling Ella Parker Santana in my arms, cooing and taking on like any typical, lovestruck new grandparent, praying her mother doesn't notice the missing hose. I'm aware nylons went out with dinosaurs, but consider me vain. I need them.

Extending my hand backward, I shove an oversized teddy bear with a bright red ribbon tied around its neck into Jack's arms.

Staring at the monstrous toy, he says calmly, "How old is she now?"

Straining to reach a smaller box that has slipped into the tire well, I return, "Four weeks — she's a month early, remember? Don't worry, she'll grow into the toy."

His clear blue gaze fixates on the gift's size. "Is the kid a Philistine?"

"Jack!" I pause to give him a humorless look. Gruff by nature, but custard on the inside, he can say the most outlandish things. "What a way to talk about your first grandbaby! Of course she isn't a giant. She'll grow into the bear."

"The thing will scar her for life." With a final scrutiny, he stacks the toy on his already burgeoning armload.

Gathering the last few items, I push the button to close the SUV hatch, and we set off for the small private airport terminal covered in winking blue and white Christmas lights. Cold wind whips the collar of my leather jacket, and I wish that I had worn my new plaid scarf. Executing a mental check, I try to recall everything that I forgot to pack for the short visit; there is always a drugstore available. I glance at Jack and snicker when I see that the top of his checkered golf hat is the only thing showing above the stacked presents.

Thank You, God, for the hundredth time. I am so blessed.

Jack's recent heart scare turned out to be a matter of having two stents inserted. But at the time that chaos was happening, Ella was making her unexpected appearance into the world, and I thought I would tear my hair out with all the uncertainties. I feared Jack's prognosis would be much worse, but an overnight stay in the hospital and he was home again, a brand-new grandfather with a clean bill of health.

I hurry to catch up and playfully pinch his ribs through his flight jacket as he walks along. Packages wobble, and he crow hops. "Arlene! Cut it out!"

He hates when I do that.

Crowding him now, I lean in for a kiss, and he complies. Honestly, I love this man more today than the day I married him. I assumed that as time passed our love would dim, but the flame only glows brighter. Not the passionate, can't-get-enough-of-you fire of youth, but a wonderful, cozy blaze lodged deep in my heart. I know without a doubt I have been one of the few who found my soul mate.

His lips taste pleasantly of cold air and the hint of the porterhouse we'd earlier devoured at Stormy's — one of Jack's favorite haunts near the terminal. "Jack, remind me to take a basket of fruit to the Graysons next week. They're such good people."

He nods. "Stick in a general gift card. I'm sure there's something they can use." Like most businessmen, Jack leaves those types of details up to me, and I am happy to comply. The restaurant owners are like family, these days. I scan the magnificent sky as we approach the company plane — one of Jack's rare extravagances. He can be tighter than a new shoe, but when it comes to planes, he throws financial caution to the wind. The beautiful Swiss-made aircraft sits waiting on the tarmac, an owner's dream. Overhead, twinkling stars welcome the impinging darkness, slight breeze — perfect night for flying.

My gaze seeks the evening star — Star of David, star of Bethlehem. I take a moment to reflect on its radiant significance. The Christ child, the most important element of Christmas.

"Merry Christmas, Mr. Santana." A terminal employee walks out to shake Jack's hand and relieve him of a few packages. "You behind the controls tonight?"

"Never miss a chance to fly, Nicky. How's that family of yours?"

"Doing great! The youngest is due any day now."

"That right? What you got this time?"

"Twins!"

"Twins." Jack shakes his head.

Nicky grins. "I know. Just what I need. I already have three under the age of five."

The men stack the presents in the rear of the eight-seater and I climb aboard. I love sitting up front with Jack. That way I can make certain he doesn't doze off. I know the autopilot is usually on, but I'm more comfortable with four eyes up front.

Jack slips the boy a bill — probably a hundred, if I know my husband — and steps aboard. The dazzling array of lighted instruments and switches gleam like diamonds in newly fallen snow. Jack once gave me a brief "Flying for Dummies" course from the new manual — things like how I would get the craft down if anything happened to him. I could land it, but it wouldn't be pretty.

Or pleasant.

Flipping a switch, he says, "Send Nicky's kids a huge box of toys for Christmas. They got twins on the way."

"I heard." *Twins!* I cringe at the thought. I adore children, but five scampering under my feet, younger than my undies? I shudder. "I'll make sure it's a big box."

Leaning sideways, my husband gives me a long, sweet kiss. When he pulls back, I stare at him, confused by the indiscreet passion in his embrace. "What's this about?"

"Ceremonial kiss for your first flight on the new craft. Plus, you might like to know that I'm crazy in love with you, that you're still the prettiest woman in the world, grandma and wife extraordinaire, and if I had to do it over, I wouldn't change one single minute of my life." He draws back. "Correction, maybe one —"

I know the reference. A black time in our marriage where precious time was wasted trying to convince ourselves that the grass was greener on the other side — which it wasn't — but it took six miserable months for us to correct the mistake.

"My, aren't we frisky tonight?" I kiss him back, caring not the least that the employee is gawking as he waits with flashlight in hand to assist our departure. Right now I am the most blessed woman on earth and I intend to enjoy every moment of this wonderful life.

There is something about night flights that's enchanting, purely whimsical. Like being on a carnival Ferris wheel, looking far down at the array of fascinating colored lights. Tonight, the twinkling golds and reds below thin, and soon the colors become more scattered. Then there is nothing but darkness. We've been in the air a little over an hour when I notice the low bank of clouds to the west. This time of year, flying always concerns me.

"Are we in for some weather?" I'd easily forgo a bumpy ride. I'm not afraid to fly — like Jack, I've been around aviation most of my life. My dad was a Navy pilot; Jack, Air Force; and both men flew during wars, so flying came as natural to me as swallowing. But I hate turbulence.

He focuses on the radar, now lit with several bright green patches. "There looks to be a small system building in the west, nothing serious."

"Good. Not that I'd mind a little snow for the season, but I can wait." Leaning back, I close my eyes, aiming to catch a little nap. This past week has been hectic, to say the least. With the holidays in full swing — shopping, wrapping gifts, scurrying from store to store — I've barely taken time to breathe.

My mind drifts to the business. Jack and I have built Santana Toys from the ground up. Three warehouses and block-long offices have grown beyond our wildest expectations, but Jack's dream to have our sons step in when we retire isn't going to happen. Our two sons instead have chosen to join their wives' family businesses. One is an electrician and the other a lawyer, and we couldn't be prouder. Both boys are happy and healthy and love what they're doing.

Jack's initial disappointment that Jack Jr. and Steven wouldn't continue his empire still hovers close to the surface, but in time, he found trusted employees who helped him grow the company into one of the largest in the United States. All said, the Santanas have a good life, and hopefully when little Ella grows up and marries, her husband will fulfill her grandfather's dream, clearly stated on our business cards: SANTANA TOYS, FAMILY OWNED AND OPERATED.

"We're picking up a little ice," Jack murmurs.

"Ice?" My eyes open.

"Nothing to worry about. This baby is capable of handling large amounts of ice." He chuckles. "Dale says the plane has a reputation for being bulletproof."

"Dale — your friend from the Air Force?" Jack has so many friends and acquaintances it's hard to keep up.

"Yeah, Dale. Everything's fine. Relax."

That's hard to do. I can see the airspeed is slowly bleeding off. Jack counteracts by adding more power.

"Everything's fine," he repeats.

The boulder-sized lump in my chest grows more pronounced, and I push the emotion aside. Closing my eyes again, I think positive. Jack is the most capable pilot I have ever flown with, and the plane is state of the art. *Nothing to be concerned about, Arlene.* I focus on the moment when I can hold baby Ella for the first time, gaze into her round, questioning eyes. Jack and I have waited five long years for our boys to start a family, and Steven and Julee finally broke the impasse.

Now the craft is rapidly gaining airspeed. My eyes fly open, and I see Jack gripping the control.

"Jack?"

"Don't be alarmed, Arlene. We're picking up a lot of ice, and it's going to stall. Hold on. It's going to be a little rocky for a few minutes."

Nodding, I sit back, panic crowding my throat as the plane descends. Apparently the weather front that had looked innocent has caught Jack off guard. What had looked to be small and nonthreatening now fills the radar screen with bright green, but the plane is new and the pilot is one of the best. *Just relax. We'll be out of this shortly.*

My heart lodges in my throat when I hear the *ding* and the wing caution device illuminates. I've been around planes long enough to know what that means: The aircraft's ice-protection system has failed.

I automatically reach for Jack's arm but can't bring myself to look at him. I feel tension straining his muscles. I can read my husband like a map, and if there is the slightest concern, I'll know by the way his brows narrow and deep lines score his forehead.

Seconds later, he speaks into his headset, talking to the closest tower. Static overrides part of the contact. "ACT, this is Pi . . . 271SMM . . . requesting . . . emergency landing . . . taking . . . heavy ice." He touches switches and sets up an emergency approach while he waits for instructions.

"It's serious, isn't it?" My voice sounds very minute and helpless, exactly like I feel. "I thought this craft was bulletproof to icing."

"Sorry — a little overstated. No plane is bulletproof to weather, but in my opinion, we're in the best craft on the market."

"Where's the nearest airstrip?"

"Not far."

My gaze traces his, and I focus on the ice flaking off the leading edges of the right wing.

"We'll be down in twenty minutes."

Jack sits back, and I note the slight slump in his posture. He can't fool me. We're in trouble. He glances over and then leans to tickle my ribs.

"Jack." I push away, aware that he is trying to ease the tension. "You know I don't like these situations."

"Who does? But we're fine."

I look out the window and see nothing but darkness below. Deep, impenetrable black. I glance at the control panels. "Am I reading this right?"

"Seems the system is building."

One glance at the radar confirms his speculation. Bright green dominates the screen. "Exactly where are we?"

"In our plane, silly girl."

I give him a no-nonsense look. "If we go down, will anyone be able to locate us?"

Solemn now, he studies the gauges. "We're about to cross the North Carolina and Virginia border."

Which means we haven't made much progress.

An intermittent voice crackles over the box, and I am barely able to make out the controller's instructions. "Pi . . . 271SM— turn right heading zero-seven-zero, maintain four thousand, five hundred . . . established. You're cleared . . . ILS runway one-zero right."

"Cleared for approach contact tower 118.1 — have a good one and thanks for the help." My husband turns and winks at me. "Cleared for approach, Milady. You can stop gripping my arm and let some blood back in my veins."

Releasing a pent-up sigh, I manage a weak smile. "I trust you."

"Sure you do — when we're not in a plane with a little ice bugging us." He puts the gear down, followed by the flaps. "I guess this means we have to spend the night in a hotel."

"I'll call the children and tell them we won't be there until morning." I put aside my immense disappointment and concentrate on the oversized teddy bear with the red ribbon around its neck sitting in the backseat. What would one night matter? Ella will be waiting when we get there.

The noise level increases, and my heart hammers. I trust my husband — if we were in real danger he would say so —

The craft lurches, and Jack shouts something — I can't catch his words, but I recognize panic in his tone.

"Jack!" We're going down. The craft is acting crazy, dropping then steadying as Jack fights the control.

I start to pray, to bargain. *Dear God, no. We're still fairly young. We have a new grandchild.* I speak for Jack, but I know his thoughts. *Let us survive to see our baby Ella — she's our only grandchild. She should be allowed to know us —*

"Arlene!" My husband's grim tone shatters my thoughts. "Are you strapped in tight?"

I am strapped so tightly I can barely breathe. The noise level in the plane is paralyzing me.

"Arlene?" He turns to meet my eyes, and I have never seen such gravity in their depths. Our gazes hold. He shouts over the engine noise. "I love you."

"Jack — no!"

The aircraft control rips free of

Jack's hands, and the plane goes into a nosedive. I can't think. I can't pray.

I am petrified.

The plane plunges, random patches of lights streak by the windshield, black sky. Lights, black sky.

Spiraling downward in a dizzying, heart-pounding plunge, I throw my arms over my head to protect my ears from a woman's terrified screams.

Chapter Two

September 12, 2015, 1:42 p.m.

Leaving Roanoke, Virginia, long-term care facility. Moving to Atlanta.

A hard rain pelts the windshield of the dark blue Lincoln as the sedan turns into an expansive mortar-and-brick complex.

A beautifully manicured landscape meets my eyes, and I focus on the large bell tower, gleaming glass, and flowering gardens. The site is incredibly peaceful after unrelenting weeks of pain and antiseptic white.

"Well, Mom, you're home." Jack Jr. half turns in the driver's seat and smiles. "What do you think?"

Nodding, I smile. I don't know what to think — or say or feel. I haven't for a long time. "What does your father think?"

The man dressed in a business suit meets the pretty woman's eyes sitting next to him. She is wearing more diamonds than a South African mine. "Mom," she says, "remember when we told you earlier that we would be taking you home today?"

I nod again. I remember. She said I was going home as soon as Jack Jr. arrived. "This isn't home."

Don't ask me how I know, but I

do. Before I left the place where I've been, I sensed something was up by the way these two had been whispering back and forth as though they shared a big secret.

Shiny gold bracelets tinkle when the woman gets out of the car and opens the back door. I sit quiet as a cornered mouse. I'm not getting out of the vehicle. This strange, rain-washed building isn't my home. I have never been clearer on that fact. I cross my arms and hunker down, prepared for a scuffle. "Tell Jack that I want to speak to him immediately."

This is so unlike my husband. Other than business trips, we have rarely been apart, and I don't appreciate the way he is avoiding me.

And the man driving the sedan? He claims to be my son Jack Jr., and the woman with the bracelets is his wife, Melissa.

Truthfully, I don't know either one of them, and I resent the way they boss me around. *"Arlene, go to dinner. Arlene, why don't you join the other ladies in the sunroom? Arlene, where is your jacket? You must eat."* They make me feel like a helpless ninny.

The people dressed in blue said that I was in an accident. I don't recall. Lately I am forced to rely on others' words. And I have no clue why the other man and woman that visit me have appointed themselves to be my younger son and his wife.

Steven and Julee who? *"We live*

fifteen minutes from the facility, Mom. I can be there in no time flat if you need something."

Live where? What would I need?

If Jack ever cuts his business trip short, I intend to find answers. Answers to why my life no longer makes sense. The whole world is nuts.

When I call for Jack, someone will say, "Dad's fine, Mom." Or "He can't be with you right now. Your job is to rest." I rest until my bones jut through my spine. Rest is the last thing I need. I want answers. Straightforward, logical facts.

If these people who appoint themselves "family" think I miss the somber expressions or lower tones, they are wrong. Their grave looks and hushed conversations frustrate me.

Melissa holds the car door open, and I stiffly flatten my body against the plush leather seat. "I am *not* going in there."

"Now Mom, we discussed this. This is the best facility in Atlanta. Don't be stubborn." Fingers with scarlet-red tips work to pry me loose from my stronghold, but I stay put. I am tired of this darkness and this constant worry about Jack, and I'm sure not going into that fancy building with all those lights.

I strengthen the hold on my crossed arms and address the man. "If you don't mind, *Mr.* Santana, I would like to go *home.*"

Killing the engine, the man steps

out of the driver's seat and walks around to the back door, his highly polished loafers sucking up rainwater. I sigh. They're going to force me in there.

Setting my jaw, I prepare to be purposely hauled out and placed on a folding wheelchair, their nondiscreet way of addressing my opposition.

Whoever these people are, I don't like them, and instinct tells me that I will find nothing of interest in that lighted mausoleum they insist I enter. My eye catches the sign over the doorway that reads SUNSET GARDENS OF BUCKHEAD. Oh joy.

If life isn't frustrating enough, I have a feeling the confusion is about to get a whole lot worse.

■ ■ ■ ■

Tiny pricks of cold rain pepper my face; thunder rolls in the distance. Car lights flash on an outer road. I can't feel my legs. Jack? Help me. Someone please help me! The plane . . . Flames . . .

Random images race through my mind. Masked faces speak above my head to the man who claims he's my son Jack Jr.

Severe head injuries . . . Amnesia, with little recall. Three broken ribs, left arm fracture . . . some paralysis which may or may not be permanent . . .

So young. Fifty-seven . . .

Ella? Where is my granddaughter, Ella Parker? Where am I?

Please, someone help. . . .

"My, aren't you an early riser?" I turn from the window to see another unfamiliar person wearing green this time.

"Did you sleep well last night?" The young blond with her hair cut in one of those uneven styles bounces over to strip the bed linens. "Bed comfy enough?"

I glance at the one thin blanket and snowy-white sheet that provides the warmth of a napkin. "May I have another blanket?"

"Sure thing." She tosses the linens on the mattress and walks out of the room, her white soles squeaking against tile. She's back carrying two neatly folded white blankets. "I brought extra. When the weather gets this warm, the air-conditioning really pumps out the cold air."

Air-conditioning. In December? In Vermont? I go along with her; I find that easier. "Yes, it does."

"Breakfast is served from six to nine, but I bet if you want a cup of coffee, the chefs won't refuse you."

"How long have I been here?" It's been months since Jack Jr. and his wife walked me to this room in this big building with the manicured lawns. I don't want to make a fuss, but I don't want to stay. Once my suitcase was unpacked and my clothing hung in the closet, the couple hadn't wanted to stay either.

The nurse opens the blinds. "Looks like the rain's over."

My gaze wanders over the unfamiliar surroundings, and I repeat, "How long have I been here?"

"I'll check in a minute, but I think you came in late yesterday." The girl fills the water pitcher sitting on the bedside stand and then pauses to admire the room. "My. This is one of the prettiest suites in the building."

I focus on the English high-back chair and matching plaid settee, highly polished table — better suited for afternoon tea than the vase of fresh-cut flowers. White stone fireplace, electric log. My bathroom adjoins the bedroom, decorated with the same muted colors. The accommodations are comfortable. "Has my husband been in today?"

"Hmm . . . I just came on shift, but I'll check with the desk as soon as I put the linens in the chute. It's still real early, Mrs. Santana."

She disappears, and I return to the window to watch the sun barely peek over the rooftops. The picture-perfect lawn glistens with morning dew. The sound of mowers in the distance faintly blends with the constant whirl of automatic sprinklers. Everything appears perfectly normal with one exception: me. Something is terribly wrong with me.

I gather enough nerve to step into the hallway a half hour later. Near-empty corridors meet my inquisitive stare. One lone woman rolls toward me in a wheelchair. My eyes focus on the perky summer hat with a red rose pinned to the front. White gloves, a white shawl around her shoulders. A massive purse sits in her lap. I glance at the pair of slacks that I'm wearing. Baggy.

I am underdressed.

When the woman draws closer, the most compelling smile breaks across her wrinkled face. "You're new here!"

Nodding, I silently concede the fact. *Stuck* is the appropriate term. "My husband is coming to take me home."

"That right?" The woman's gaze assesses me. "Who said?"

"I say."

"They all say that. Well, honey"

— she hooks a free arm through mine — "the name's Gwendolyn."

"I am Arlene."

"Arlene. Good enough for me. Come along, the eggs are worse when they're cold."

My feet fly along the hallway, and I manage to keep up with the rolling chair. This is more exercise than I've had in . . . well, I don't know how long, but this is work.

"How long are you in for?"

"Pardon?"

"How long? Rehab, recovery, or hauled out on a morgue stretcher?"

I pick one. "Recovery." Room numbers fly by me. "Can you slow down?"

"You need to pick up speed, girl."

I would gladly eat cold food in

exchange for a second to catch my breath.

"The facility is a nice place to visit, but nobody wants to live here," Gwendolyn informs me. "Come on. I'll introduce you to the gang."

We turn the corner, and I half run into a spacious dining area with crystal chandeliers, fancy plates, and cups and saucers. Two women sit to the right at a round, white-covered table wearing blank expressions.

"Howdy, gals." Gwendolyn rolls to the table and motions for me to have a seat. "We have a newbie. This is Arlene. She's going to sit at our table."

"Does she have permission?" the

lady in a fuchsia blouse asks.

Rolling her eyes, Gwendolyn snaps, "At these prices, she can run the joint if she wants."

Eyes slowly lift to acknowledge me. I don't think I've ever seen a sadder assortment of expressions. Life has been sucked from sockets.

Summoning a pleasant smile, I return, "Good morning, ladies."

I choose the seat closest to Gwendolyn, hoping the tablemates aren't the chatty sort. Someone eases a menu in front of me, and I study my choices. The selections read like the Waldorf Astoria's Peacock Room Sunday brunch menu. My eyes bug when I note the chocolate fountain. I close the folder. "One scrambled egg, buttered toast, and coffee with cream."

The four of us sit in a strained silence, awaiting our meal. Finally the lady wearing a gold blouse and oversized hooped earrings introduces herself as Eleanor. The woman beside her, wearing a dark wig that casts shadows on the map of wrinkles across her face, says, "Frances."

Gwendolyn chatters like a magpie. "What you in for, honey? You're awfully young."

I sit up straighter when I realize that I am being spoken to. "Oh. Amnesia — I'm told. I don't recall."

The women chuckle, bringing a brush of warmth to my cheeks. I suppose I can manage a better response, but my mind goes blank in the middle of a sentence.

Gwendolyn must notice my discomfort because she stops laughing. "Aw, honey, we're not laughing at you, we're laughing with you. Nobody around here can remember squat."

The good-natured response puts me more at ease. Unfolding my white linen napkin, I place it in my lap. "I am told that I was involved in an accident, and the injuries affect a certain part of my brain — the part that . . . knows things."

Eleanor nods. "Wake up to new world every day? Welcome to the club. I'm told I'm getting dementia."

Every last one at the table understands my confusion. Frances says, "Shoot, I can't remember if I'm coming, or if I've already been there. I have more aches and pains than Carter has liver pills."

"I don't think they make those pills anymore." Eleanor laces her coffee with heavy cream. "Or maybe they do."

Gwendolyn agrees with an affirmative nod. "Carter's Little Liver Pills. Who can forget them?"

I could. I never heard of the pills, but judging more by sense than knowledge, I think I must be much younger than these women. As though Eleanor is a mind reader, she asks, "How old are you, Arlene?"

Resting my spoon on the edge of

my cup, I shake my head. "I don't know."

"You look to be in your middle to late fifties."

I am in my midfifties. Good to know. I accept the age. "All right."

During the meal, I keep my eye on the man at the end of the corridor. From my vantage point, I can see down two long passages. He is in corridor one, crouching in front of the outside door, holding a pair of pliers as he inches back and forth in front of the door frame.

"Have you noticed the man in that corridor?" I ask.

Eleanor glances up. "You talking about Frank?"

"I don't know his name, but I fear he's trying to open the door and needs help."

"He can't open the door. They keep an alarm on it. Frank's a former electrician. He's trying to figure out the code, so he can break out."

Somehow I get the drift. "Oh my." I would never be that daring. Or would I?

"Don't worry. The staff changes the code every few days." Gwendolyn picks up her napkin and pats her lips. Rummaging in her large purse, she snags a tube of bright red lipstick and reapplies color. When she notices me watching, she silently offers me the tube. I shake my head. I am fairly confident that I wouldn't be caught dead wearing that particular shade.

Shrugging, she applies another coat, rolling her lips together several times to smooth the effect. "Better watch them electricians, sweetie. There's a lot of 'em around."

Later, I wander back to my room, taking time to explore cubbyholes and a few closed doors. My surroundings are quite opulent, but the people who dwell here wear the same hopeless expressions. A wave of loneliness swamps me. Where is Jack? Where are my sons? My family has left me here, alone and defenseless.

In one hall, I spot a doctor wearing a white coat, giving a patient what looks to be an optical examination. I hear him say, "Now Mr. Denton, I want you to put your right hand over your right eye."

"Okay."

"Good. Then you'll put your left hand over your left eye." The doctor fidgets with an instrument.

The man obeys, and I pause to watch.

"Now read me what comes after the large *E.*"

The man shakes his head. "Can't."

"Try, sir. I need the letter directly below the big *E.*"

"Can't do it. Can't see a blame thing."

The doctor straightens. The man has both eyes covered.

Nodding to the doctor, I walk on,

feeling even more confident that I'm not going to like it here and nothing I've encountered so far changes my mind.

Chapter Three

Year One

Eleanor's prophetic guess proves to be spot-on. I do wake to a new world every day. I eat the same breakfast with the same faces, see the same nurses and janitors, and every new day life feels as if I am back to square one. Bill Murray's movie *Groundhog Day* flashes through my mind, and I wonder if I am stuck in a time warp. Odd that the memory of that movie stood out in my mind.

Reluctant to get up this morning, I stare at the two new pictures on my wall and wonder why the staff feels the need to change wall decor so often. Every morning a new hanging or painting is tacked on my living room wall. The service seems a bit over the top but the items are interesting to contemplate. I don't recognize any of the bright, shining smiles, but they must mean something to me.

The only thing I know for certain is Gwendolyn is friendly and that I can trust her. I don't care for bead making, Bingo, or ring toss, and I have been here long enough for loneliness to set in, a hollow melancholy ache that grips my insides and makes me think that I've been nibbling on too many green apples.

I am pretty decent at napkin folding.

When Gwendolyn discovers that, like her, I am an early riser, she stops by the room each morning and insists that I fold napkins with her. I don't mind. What else is there to do at 4:30 a.m.?

Jack Jr. and Steven tell me they come twice a week for visits, but they don't. They haven't been here in ages. Just two couples that I don't recognize stop in once in a while, and if they can spare the time, they take me outside for fresh air. They must work here, though I've never thought to ask.

They don't fold napkins.

Gwendolyn tells me the couple is

my son and daughter-in-law and they often spend an hour rolling my chair among the dying flower beds and colorful falling leaves. They tell me that one of my sons lives in Vermont and the other in Georgia. My tablemate says Steven is closer and visits more often, but I can't say. I'm still confident it's only a matter to time before my Jack comes to take me home.

CHAPTER FOUR

Year Two

The corridors fill with plump, round pumpkins wearing carved faces. The pretty sight lines the hallways. I give "Dr. Important" a rude notice when he sweeps by in his perpetual, all-fired-hurry stride. I can't imagine why the man lives life in such a frantic rush. It's all I can do to pass twenty-four hours.

In truth, I am envious. I wish I had somewhere to go that urgently.

Gwendolyn and the girls are

seated and waiting for me as I approach the dining room table. An occasional nurse smiles and says good morning when we pass, but the residents are engrossed in their food. I slide into my chair and pause a moment to admire Gwendolyn's hat. "Is that a peacock feather?"

Gwendolyn preens. "Why yes, it is. Thank you for noticing. The hat belonged to my mother."

"Most lovely."

"The shawl was Mother's, too."

I make the appropriate clucking over the lovely crocheted white yarn that has been discussed before, I think. The eyestrain-causing work must have taken long hours to complete.

"My grandpapa purchased the hat for Mother on her sixteenth birthday."

"A very thoughtful gift," Frances says.

I notice the women eat rather quickly this morning except for Frances, who I've discovered can stretch her nibbling of a simple piece of toast like a fussy toddler.

"Does anyone know why the staff changes the wall art so often?" I sample my omelet — add a sprinkle of salt and pepper. Frances slowly lifts her gaze from her plate.

I go on to explain. "In the mornings when I open my eyes, there's a new family picture or painting on the wall. I lie for long moments, trying to identify the images of smiling faces — but I can't say who anyone is."

I have grown accustomed to strange faces, but why would the staff hang pictures of strangers in my room? When I mention the oddity about the images to the man who identifies himself as "Steven," he says he will ask the nurses, but the rotating pictures continue.

"Oh, those pictures." Gwendolyn taps artificial sweetener over her oatmeal. "It's Simon. The poor thing belongs in the Alzheimer's unit, but somehow he manages to slip out and hang the pictures that he takes from other rooms. Don't mind Simon. He's harmless."

I nod. I understand her answer. It's the apparent norm that confuses me. But the hangings aren't bothersome. They make the room more interesting.

"People seem in a bit of a hurry this morning." I dab a half spoon of apple jelly on my plate, failing to see what has their interest.

"We get our costumes today," Eleanor says.

I glance up. "Is there a ball?" Nothing — and I do mean nothing — surprises me around here.

"No, today is Halloween." Gwendolyn leans closer. "You do remember Halloween, don't you? Costumes. Candy. Trick or treat?"

"Of course I recall the . . ." I search for a word. "Publicity."

I don't recognize the word *Halloween,* but Gwendolyn makes the event sound like a big deal, and I want in.

"Candy? I got sticky, unwrapped popcorn balls," Frances grouses.

"Same here — and pieces of broken cookies." Eleanor bites into a prune.

"The fudge was tasty," Gwendolyn admits. "When I get new teeth, I'm going to tell my daughter to put nuts in mine this Christmas."

Eleanor shakes her head. "Sad those days have passed. Today's parent is forced to lead the toddlers to neighborhood parking lots and let them select their treats from the back of a car or pickup truck. I imagine it's the same old Tootsie Pops and Skittles, year after year after year."

"You mentioned costumes?" I might have lost my mind, but I still know everyone at the table is much too old to be trick-or-treating.

"Arlene, you were here last year." Gwendolyn pauses. "I forget, you were new last year, and you didn't come out of your room for the party." She pats my shoulder. "This year you'll be joining the fun. The staff will hand out costumes shortly and assign stations."

I'm sure my expression is as blank as air. All this chatter about costumes and suckers. I can't follow the conversation. I wave Eleanor's offer of a prune away.

"Everyone gets to be something special on Halloween," Gwendolyn says. “The place that you want to shoot for is the main entrance. If you nail that one, you get the Cinderella costume and hand out candy at the front door. The families and employees bring their small children through the facility. It’s a special night.”

I shake my head. “I have nothing to give them.” I still haven’t found my purse.

“Don’t worry, the nurses supply the candy. It’s a riot.”

I focus on her excitement, trying to imagine myself dressed as Cinderella. “Do you want to be Cinderella this year?”

“I wish.” Gwendolyn sighs. “I got to be her last year. I’ll be stuck with either Red Riding Hood or the fox but I don't care."

"Now Gwendolyn, you know that's a fib." Frances glances my way. "*She* wants to be Cinderella. Every woman in here wants the position, but we have to share."

Eleanor nibbles on her toast. "I was a chicken last year."

"You were a *rooster,*" Gwendolyn corrects. "There is a difference."

My eyes ping-pong back and forth, trying to follow the conversation. Chickens. Roosters. I want to contribute something to the inane conversation, but I'm blank.

"Hush up, Gwendolyn. You get to do everything. High time you set back and take your turn."

Was that a touch of petulance in Frances's tone?

Gwendolyn's chin lifts for battle. "You can fold napkins for the chefs, too, if you'd get up early enough. You're just jealous."

"What about the popcorn?" Frances asks.

The two women's forks pause in midair like battle shields coming up.

I hurry to change the subject. I am not accustomed to confrontations. Jack and I rarely lift our voices to each other, not since our children left home. "Ladies," I caution.

Other residents start to stare.

"So?" Gwendolyn challenges. "I work hard to get that position. It's mine."

Eleanor bends closer. "Ignore

them. Popcorn is a touchy subject around here."

"Why so?" I can't imagine why there is such crackling tension over a bag of popped corn.

Eleanor's eyes dart to the sparring pair. "Gwendolyn got the corn-popping job for Bingo games a couple of years ago when Laverne . . . suddenly departed. Frances holds a grudge. She wants the job."

I guess I understand the disagreement, but the idea of two grown women squabbling over corn seems petty and pointless. The whole conversation enforces my original thoughts. I want out of here.

After breakfast, I trail the women

to corridor one for the costume distribution. Gwendolyn insists that I participate. If the subject of corn upsets the women, I shudder to think how they'll react if I refuse a costume, so I go.

The following hour consists of endless squabbles, hair pulling, shoving and high-pitched squeals. Somehow I lose a shoe, and I'm never able to locate it. My head throbs. And my toes. An irate eighty-year-old brings her cane solidly down on my right foot, on my toes, and I think she breaks the middle one. When the dust settles, the women clutch their spoils to their chests and make a beeline for their rooms. Gwendolyn proudly carries the Red Riding Hood dress, though she denies that she knocked Shelly Middleton off her feet to get it.

I, on the other hand, feel like an intruder when the Cinderella costume accidently lands in my arms, and I find myself acting as selfish as the others. During a scuffle impasse, someone loses her false teeth, and I think, *Ew! What am I doing here?*

A white-haired lady jerks the Cinderella dress from my hands, and I jerk right back. Hard. Two can play this game.

Fabric rips, and a nurse steps in to break up the fracas.

But fair is fair, and I latch onto the costume. Hugging the musty-smelling cloth to my chest, I straighten, and with as much dignity as possible, I lopsidedly walk back down the hallway. I need my other shoe, but I'll get it later.

Safely inside my room, I slip the dress over my head and parade before the full-length mirror. I don't recognize the image of the older woman with mussed hair and a missing sneaker. It sure isn't me, but nonrecognition is the norm nowadays. The garment fits perfectly, and I have to admit that the costume is adorable.

For the first time in a very long time, hope springs anew, and the thick gray veil of darkness that has draped me in despair slowly starts to lift. Perhaps there is hope for me. I am Cinderella.

I actually look forward to the Halloween event tonight.

The festivities start early. Perching on a bar stool, I sit on my throne and hand out candy. Sticky fingers and cherubic grins meet my efforts, and I find myself smiling — even laughing when eager hands grab more than their share.

Candy is flowing when Steven and Julee (the couple who claim they are my younger son and daughter-in-law) come through the line. I realize that I have not thought about anyone I know coming to the party, but the darling little girl they carry in their arms is about the cutest thing I've ever seen. Long, dark blond hair; big round blue eyes; maybe two years old; and wearing a Tinker Bell costume, even down to the lovely green slippers. My heart melts like ice cream on a summer sidewalk when the child leans out to give me a big smack on my right cheek.

"My goodness! I believe this calls for two pieces of candy!" The spot where her lips touched feels warm and most likely gummy. And precious. Her baby scent fills my senses, and I draw deep of the Fountain of Youth.

"Steven," I chide, hoping I have the name right, "who is this lovely child?"

"Mom . . ." He glances at Julee. "This is Ella — your grandbaby."

"Ella?" My smile wanes to a cold

stare. My grandbaby — baby Ella? Anger impedes my throat, and I spring to my feet. Candy spills to the floor. "Steven! Why would you fib to me and say this child is my Ella! My Ella is a newborn — this child is *not.*"

His gaze drops, and he changes the subject. "Hey little girl. Look at all the candy!"

I bend to rescue the candy that smaller children scramble to stuff in bags and orange buckets. My hands shake. *Why would Steven mislead me when he knows how I long to see my grandbaby?* I straighten to face him. "Don't do that to me again. Ever."

"Sorry, Mom." He hefts the little girl higher. "Want some candy from the nice lady? It's all right to take it."

I grudgingly fish in my basket and find a couple of bags of Skittles. Not that the child isn't adorable, but no one is going to replace my Ella.

Nobody better try.

"Well, she is special, Steven," I allow. "I have a new grandbaby — she's six weeks old, and her name is Ella Parker. I'm going to meet her soon." Julee hands me a tissue, and I wipe my eyes. I can't recall ever getting this upset. I must be getting better.

"That's wonderful, Mom. I'm sure she's adorable."

"Ohhh . . . oh yes! You can have candy, too!" I laugh when eager hands compel Steven, Julee, and the little girl farther down the line. I glance back, fascinated with the angel Steven carries in his arms. Someday I'll carry my Ella like that.

The child's memory stays with me long after the treats are gone and the front doors are locked for the night. I lie in my bed, watching a flurry of colorful dry leaves skip across the lighted parking lot. Baby Ella. I haven't thought about my grandchild in a while. There's so much going on — so many changes. Has Jack phoned Steven to tell him that we are detained by ice?

"The plane is sound. Nothing to worry about, Arlene."

Words form in the darkness. "But

I do worry, Jack. I want you to come home — I want to go *home* with you and sit before our fire and feel alive again."

"Good night, Milady."

"Good night, my love." Yawning, I roll to my side and close my eyes. Being Cinderella is fun. Maybe next year I'll have to be the rooster, but there are worse things in life.

As I drift off, thunder sounds in the distance, and a soft rain patters against the windowpane.

Today hasn't been so bad, Arlene. Maybe you're yodeling. . . . No, that isn't the word. Clocking. That's it, I'm clocking.

Or is that, coping?

Chapter Five

Year Three

Rehab. Now there's a place that strikes fear in you. I have to bat a silly balloon around, lift a few small weights, and touch my toes while I'm sitting down. This morning a nurse remarks, "Arlene, I bet you worked out before the accident. You're in pretty good shape."

"I do," I say, hefting twice the weight of the others. "Nine days a week." Jack and I are fitness freaks. We ride bikes on long Sunday afternoons, play tennis. Jack even belongs to the racquetball club. The nurse's remark brightens my morning because to me it looks like my body is falling apart. Loose skin. Pulled-pork underarms. I lower the weight and study my right forearm. Once smooth, soft skin now resembles parchment paper — either that or I am wearing a garment in bad need of ironing.

A man wearing a doctor's coat almost runs me over when he hurries down the hallway. I've seen the man before, always in a rush as though he is needed at a fire. He was in the dining room this morning, and Gwendolyn said that everyone thinks that he is a smart aleck. Even I have started to call him "Dr. Important" behind his back, which I'm aware isn't nice.

I step aside and watch him stride to the nurse's station and leisurely pick up a copy of the morning newspaper and peruse the headlines.

My gaze focuses on his shiny leather loafers. Dr. Important is the kind one would like to see wearing scuffed shoes and baggy trousers to make him more likeable. Maybe he'd even bend over someday and turn into Refrigerator Man. That would be funny.

But not today. Everything is in place. Tasteful. Fastidious.

Perhaps if he ever took the time to speak, to say, "Excuse me, Arlene," like most of the staff did, I would like him more.

Angry voices filter from my room when I approach. A man and woman — their voices restrained to a civil level but sharp. "Get off my back, Melissa. I'm doing the best that I can."

"You? What about me, Jack? What about *me.* Do you think these past years have been a piece of cake? I told you it would be easier to bring her to our house. She is never going to be happy here. And the inconvenience you've brought upon the whole family is intolerable. We'll remodel a couple of rooms and hire a private nurse. The Lord knows our house can use a change."

"And let her die of loneliness and neglect? How often are you home for any length of time, Melissa? Once — maybe twice a week? She loves people, and she'll wither away in our stuffy crypt."

"Are you insinuating that our home is cold?" The woman's voice has assumed an icy likeness.

I pause some twenty feet away from the doorway to allow a man mopping the floor to slide his cleaning bucket aside.

"I didn't ask for this," Jack Jr.'s voice reminds her. "Do you think managing the toy business and my office in Vermont *and* commuting to long-standing clients and my partners in Atlanta is easy?"

"How would I know? You never talk to me about anything these days, and you've missed the last two counseling sessions. I can't recall the last time we worshipped together. Or made love."

"I'm one person. I don't need a pastor or a high-priced shrink to tell me that I have a problem."

"We, Jack. *We* have a problem, and I am trying my best to correct it, but I can't if you refuse to cooperate. If you can't bear the sight of me, then maybe we should separate." Her tone softens. "That isn't what I want, and I don't believe you want it either. Don't give up on this marriage, Jack. I haven't."

"Love. The most highly overrated sentiment in the English language. Love cannot heal all problems, Melissa. Grow up and live in the real world."

The janitor moves on, yet I hesitate. Something is wrong. Terribly wrong. I wonder if I should interrupt what sounds like a private conversation.

The woman's soft voice drifts to me. "Is there another woman?"

"There isn't another woman. I have a woman. I don't need another headache."

"That's what I am now? A headache?"

"This is not the place to have this discussion, Melissa. Mother will be here anytime."

The woman's tone cools. "You aren't being fair, Jack. I do my part in this marriage. You're the one who slaves twenty hours a day, refusing to take a break, ignores family life, and goes out of your way to avoid your wife. I know you're overwhelmed with losing your father, with work, and your mother's illness, but I do everything possible to make your losses easier —"

"Easier? Be serious. I barely have time to eat these days."

Her tone drops to menacing. "Don't tell me you aren't going to be there. Julee has the turkey in the oven, the table is set and guests invited — the Johnsons are coming this year. It was your idea to have Julee invite them. You can't leave me to entertain alone."

"The Johnsons are your friends, not mine."

"What a horrible thing to say! You

know I wouldn't associate with them if they didn't provide your law office a healthy income every year. You *told* me to invite them."

His tone rises. "Make *my* apologies."

"You *make* room for the things that are important to *you.* Somehow you manage to show up for golf dates."

"You're right. When you're in yoga five times a week and most Saturdays, I'm on the golf course trying to close a deal. Try having responsibilities, Melissa, like running two businesses —"

I've heard enough. Whatever the problem, this anger has to stop. Broadcasting one's problems through the corridors is no solution. Summoning a smile, I step into the room, pretending great surprise to see company. "My goodness! I see that I have guests."

Jack Jr. turns from the window and offers a strained smile. "Happy Thanksgiving, Mom."

"Thanksgiving?" This part still confuses me. I have celebrated Thanksgiving already. Jack bought a roasted hen at the market, and I tossed a salad. Later we dozed in our recliners. But I've learned to smile and nod when someone says something mystifying. "The same to you." I turn to the woman. "So nice to see you, Julee."

"Melissa," she gently corrects and bends to hug me. Gold bracelets tinkle, and a lovely scent enfolds me. Elizabeth Taylor's Passion. Judging by the woman's smell, we've met before.

"Please." I gesture to the sofa. "Sit with me awhile."

The couple settles on the sofa at a safe distance, and we chat about inane things. How nice to have the weather hold. Yes, the facility was quite comfortable, but I miss my home. I ache for my comfy bed. The familiar feel of Jack lying next to me at night, moonlight streaming through our bedroom window.

"Have you made any new friends this month?" the woman inquires.

"Oh yes." I tell her about Gwendolyn. And Eleanor and Frances, but by her squirmy expression, I think I might have mentioned the tablemates before.

Jack Jr. lifts a brow. "Surely you meet many people here. Not just Gwendolyn, Eleanor, and Frances."

"Not really. There are a lot of people here, and they're okay, but I don't associate — I don't think. But if you want, I'll try harder."

I should tell him that I prefer to sit in my room and gaze out the window in lovely silence more than listen to the inane babble that goes on here. I play games like car counting — how many white vehicles come and go each day? Make up stories about the owners and their lives, where they're going when they leave here. Total the amount of falling leaves when a wind gust drops dying foliage. I counted fourteen squirrels skimming across the ground this morning — but one kept running back and forth. . . .

So I started over.

"You need to socialize more, Mom. The nurses say that you stay in your room too much." He checks his shiny gold watch.

"Friends help pass the time," Melissa encourages.

"I try, but often the conversations around me don't make any sense." I lean in. "Some of these people aren't all there — if you know what I mean."

Melissa solemnly nods. "I understand."

She's a nice girl. "But all is well," I assure. I sit back and relax. This is a most pleasant visit. For the first time in a long time, I feel that I have something to contribute to the conversation.

I look up. "Where is Jack?"

The man and woman exchange tolerant looks. "Now Mom, I've explained. Dad is going to be away for a while. He wants you to know that he loves you and for you to relax and enjoy life."

Enjoy *this* life? Jack can't be serious. That would be the same as lying back and enjoying a good case of malaria. What is he thinking? "Where did he go that he has to stay so long?"

The man glances at the woman.

"Oh. I'll bet he went to Australia," I muse. "We have a large account there, and he said we need to visit the customer."

The woman releases a sigh. "That must be it. He didn't actually say where he was going."

"No," I retract. "He wouldn't go to Australia without me. We are planning to make that trip a very long vacation, and he wouldn't go without me."

Jack Jr. suddenly stands up and walks to the window. "Hey, Steven said that he and Julee plan to visit this afternoon."

"Steven? Why that's wonderful. I haven't seen Steven in ages. Is he well? And baby Ella. My goodness, she must be twelve weeks old now, and I have yet to see the little dumpling. Tell Steven to bring her by anytime. I can have company — all the guests that I want." Pausing, my mind goes blank, and I try to think of what I need to say. The bear. Where did I put the toy? "Your father thinks the bear is way too big for her, but I told him that she'll grow into the toy."

"Steven's fine," Jack says.

"Have you seen it?"

"The bear?"

"Yes."

"I . . . I've seen a bear. Hey Mom, want to go outside before we leave?"

"No, we'll visit right here."

Time flies so swiftly that a rush of letdown fills me when the man reaches for his coat. "Hate to rush, Mom, but I have to stop by the office and put in a few hours before dinner." His gaze avoids the woman named Melissa.

"So soon?" I get up to walk the couple to the door. Earlier he told the woman that he wasn't coming home for dinner tonight. Why would Jack Jr. fib to me? I smile at the lady. "I like your bracelets. They're so pretty. Did you buy them here in Vermont?"

"No . . ." She glances at the man. "Actually, they are a gift from my mother-in-law."

"Well, she certainly has lovely taste."

"I've always thought so." She bends to embrace me. "Take care of yourself. We'll be back soon."

"Visit anytime," I urged. "I'm

never busy."

"We will. Soon."

They always say that. They won't come.

"Have a good holiday," the man says.

"You, too!"

Chapter Six

Later, I am weary from trying to make new friends. The nurse said I could eat supper at a different table with people I didn't know. Gertrude, Eleanor, and Frances were a bit miffed, but after I explained that Jack Jr. said I had to make other friends, they said that I could sit where I wanted. I choose a lovely couple well up in years, and the choice seems to please them. We eat pumpkin pie, and the woman dribbles whipped cream on her chin. I am tempted to whisk it away with my napkin, but I keep my hands to myself. You never know how anyone is going to take simple manner correction around here. This particular woman is known to be cranky and doesn't know up from down. But then neither do I.

I spend the rest of the evening alone, sitting in my armchair, counting car lights.

It isn't the best Thanksgiving ever. I fondly remember the hearty celebrations I experienced as a child. I come from a large family with three sisters and five brothers, and I can't think of a time that we didn't spend the holidays together, usually at my grandmother's house when I was small, and then later at the oldest sibling's house when my mother and father turned the holiday duties over to Susie, who did little more than set a pretty table.

Jack and I would stay up most of Thanksgiving and Christmas Eve, baking hams and turkeys and peeling enough potatoes for forty-two people. By the time we fell into bed in the wee hours of the morning, the most delectable aroma scented the house. Thanksgiving Day was the topper. Somehow my sisters and I had fallen into the Black Friday madness, so instead of bed we had an official family bunking party on Thanksgiving night. After several pots of strong Maxwell House, we would dress warmly and hope to be among the first twenty people in line for the Friday bargains. Everyone knew the seventy-five-inch wide-screen smart television advertised for $199.00 would be gone in a flash, that in truth there was only one in the store at that price, but we didn't care. I could always use another ten-dollar Crock-Pot.

The men went along with the craziness, standing close to the checkout lanes when we rushed by and transferred stacks of "must have" bargains. Who couldn't use another wok?

Jack and I decided long ago that whatever we saved during those mad rushes wasn't worth the effort, but it wasn't slashed prices that drew us; it was the bonding.

Sighing, I switch off the light and crawl into bed. A soft glow from the grounds' security lights filters through the curtains.

Closing my eyes, I say my daily prayer. "God, thank You for today's blessings, for food and shelter. Wherever Jack is, please keep him safe and bring him home to me, soon."

I know that I am well cared for and not forgotten. Still, longing fills my every waking hour, the kind of ache that only my former life can diminish. Deep down where the pain is the worst, I know that I can't go back.

Removing my glasses, I lay them on the bedside table and hunker down for another long night.

Snow drifts from a leaden sky. I sit in the craft room beading a necklace. I've told Gwendolyn a hundred times that I don't like crafty activities, but honestly, the days are long, and if making a necklace passes time, I'd agree to hog washing for distraction. The halls teem with activity today. Pumpkins disappear, and workers line the corridors, hanging strings of garland and festive lights.

"We can help decorate the tree, if we want." The woman sitting beside me slides another white bead onto a thin wire.

"Really?" The news brings no great sense of satisfaction, only the knowledge that the facility is finally catching up to my time. The holiday was only a few weeks away before the accident, and I was in the hospital maybe . . . Well, that I didn't know, but regardless, it didn't seem possible Christmas could come twice in one month.

I shake my head. I've stopped trying to figure out the jigsaw puzzle called life. "I love the holidays."

"You have to get there early. The snow geese grab the elephants," the woman sitting at the end says.

I eye the woman and mentally sigh. I've sat with this one before. She mumbles.

Snow geese.

Elephants.

Scooping up my beads, I slide to

the end of the table where Gwendolyn works. "That lady down there says we get to help decorate the Christmas tree."

Engrossed in her work, Gwen — as Gwendolyn now insists we call her, silently nods.

"That should be fun." At least the activity would be something she enjoys.

We work in silence as snow drifts gently down on the complex roof. Finally I mention, "I think Jack will be home for Christmas." Smiling, I recall the times when we selected our tree. We'd bundle up tightly, laughing like kids as we drove to the Christmas tree farm. We selected our tree a year before purchasing it and often came to the farm in the summer to judge its growth. Some grew to a magnificent height, while other years we'd gotten the runt. We never complained. I had never seen an ugly pine lit with twinkling lights and colorful tinsel.

Jack prefers multicolored bulbs with popcorn strings, none of those "theme" trees. We'd drink hot chocolate and hang ornaments that meant something to us. The kids' amateur school efforts: Merry Christmas, Mommy and Daddy; Jack Jr.'s first tooth encased in plastic; Steven's black horn-rimmed frames from his first pair of glasses. I paid to have our wedding certificate made into a lovely ornament that hung beside the beautiful star of Bethlehem that crowned the treetop in glorious fashion. Our Christmas tree was a tribute to the Santanas' lives and to the Savior the star represented.

The tree was as clear in my mind this morning as though I was standing in front of it.

"Psst."

I glance in the direction of the sound and frown when I see Frances half crouching in the doorway, her bent frame wavering. She jerks her head for me to come meet her.

Pushing my beads aside, I send Gwen a curious glance and push back my plastic chair. When I reach the doorway, Frances jerks me into the hall. I never imagined that the spindly little spinster has that much strength.

"Hey." I break the grip of her hand on my blouse.

"I need your help."

"Me?"

"You're tall. Come with me."

I didn't think of myself as tall. Or someone to be jerked about like a hangman's noose. "Let go of my blouse."

She half drags me to the area where the private mailboxes are kept. The BE BACK SOON sign is propped on the counter. I size up the situation and turn to look at her. "What?"

"Get my mail."

I turn back to the closed counter. "I can't. The lady's gone."

"You're light and much younger

than me. Climb over the counter and get my mail. There's an envelope in my slot."

I have never, in my limited memory, ever climbed over anything containing a sign that read CLOSED.

"You do it. You're the circus performer."

"My family was. I worked the ropes and net."

"I am not going to climb over the counter, Frances. There are rules that we must obey. You do it."

"Can't. I can't lift my leg high enough to heft myself over."

"No!" Gwendolyn and Eleanor are always in hot water over one of Frances's indiscretions. Frances is the resident rebel, and I am not a troublemaker.

"No," I repeat more calmly, adding a note of finality. Frances can't make me.

"Then give me a shove up." She lifts a spindly leg and latches on to her ankle.

"You will *not* climb up there," I whisper harshly. My gaze skims the busy hallway. "You'll hurt yourself." She's wobbling around like a crazed chicken on one foot.

"My pension check is in that slot. I need it." Frances falls against the mail counter and freezes, still holding her ankle.

"You don't need your check bad enough to break a bone. You're not going anywhere." I hate to be the bearer of bad news, but I'm not going to scale the counter like a chimpanzee. She doesn't need that check. I overheard someone complain that it was only Monday. The shuttle bus didn't operate on Mondays.

"I'm going over." Frances drops her ankle and faces me defiantly. "If you won't get it, I will."

Now what? Allow her to climb up there and break something, or get her silly mail myself? I should report her to a nurse, but tattletales are dead meat around here. It's clear that she isn't taking no for an answer.

"Come on — I'll take the blame if we get caught."

"We?" I ask.

"I'll take the blame. Just do it!"

"All right." I risk a second glance down the hallway and assure myself that nobody is watching. "I'll get it."

Toeing off my shoes, I wet my lips and prepare to make a quick postal stop. I slap Frances's hand away when she offers a hand up. "Stop it! I can do this."

With a mighty leap, I heft myself over the counter and then easily drop to the opposite side. Frances's voice trails me.

"While you're in there you might as well get Gwen's mail, too. Her check is due today."

"Don't *even* ask," I hiss between closed teeth. My gaze travels the long row of slots and pauses on a magazine sticking out of Frank

Mettle's opening. Squinting, I focus on the racy cover with a voluptuous woman wearing an underwire garment that doesn't fit. Why, the old geezer!

"Hurry up!" Frances's voice forces my eyes to move on. I spot her slot and grab the lone envelope. When I straighten and turn around, I come face-to-face with a nurse. Perilea R. Reynolds, RN. Frances is nowhere in sight.

"Arlene?"

Smiling, I say brightly, "Yes?"

"What are you doing behind the mail counter? You know that's against the rules."

"Yes I know."

"Well?"

"I . . . need my mail," I lie.

"Arlene." The nurse slowly wags her head. "I wish I could let this pass with a warning — you've been the ideal patient — but we can't have our residents climbing over counters. You could hurt yourself, and we are responsible for our patients' well-being."

"Yes, Miss Reynolds. I'm sorry. I was getting Frances's mail." I don't know what else to say but the truth.

She shakes her head as though I am making up stories. "Please come with me."

"Yes ma'am." I fall into step behind her, and we march down corridor one. When I round the corner, a wrinkled hand snakes out and snatches the check from my clutch. I whirl and shoot Frances a disgusted look before she darts away.

A pleasant young woman, younger than springtime, sits behind a desk with a gold nameplate: CANDACE L. MARSHALL, ADMINISTRATOR. She glances up when I follow the nurse into the office.

"Have a seat, Arlene."

I timidly sit down and cross my hands. Humiliation drips from my pores. I focus on the girl's flawless makeup, and the inane thought crosses my mind to inquire which foundation she uses.

"Well Arlene." Long scarlet nails tap a manila folder. "I understand that you've been climbing counters this morning."

I slowly nod my head. "Frances told me to get her mail."

"Frances?"

"My tablemate."

"Go on."

"She needs her social security check."

"We have an attendant that works the mail counter."

"She wasn't there."

"So you volunteered to get the check for her?"

"No." I don't recall the incident happening that way. "Frances threatened to climb the counter herself, and I thought that she might hurt herself. So I climbed it."

Sighing, Candace closes the folder. "I'm going to let you off with a warning, Arlene. Do *not* climb anything in the facility. If you need help, you will ask an employee for assistance."

Like an employee would scale the counter for Frances's mail? Nobody but the attendant carries the mail key. "Yes ma'am."

"Very well. Have a nice day."

I leave my chair and reach for the door handle when instinct tells me to ask, "Does this mean I can still help decorate the tree tonight?"

"Yes, of course you can help decorate. Have a good time."

"Thank you. One more thing."

"Yes?"

"What foundation do you use?"

Surprise crosses the woman's features. "It's bareMinerals. Why?"

"It's pretty — you look pretty."

"Thank you, Arlene. You look very nice yourself."

Quietly closing the door, I vow it will be a cold day in you-know-where before I offer to get anybody's mail again. Plus, I plan to wring Frances's scrawny neck the next time I see her.

Chapter Seven

During dinner, Frances is quiet as a mouse and refuses to meet my accusing gaze, but even the prickly tension can't overshadow the air of expectancy. The tree decorations sit around the massive holiday fir awaiting tinsel, helping hands, and blinking lights.

Gwendolyn sneezes a couple of times before dessert, and I hand her a tissue. "Thanks. I hope I'm not coming down with a cold."

"When I was little," Frances ventures, chewing with her mouth open. "I always got sick just before Christmas. I don't know if anticipation caused it or I was merely puny, but whatever, I came down with something on Christmas Eve. The year I got my first pair of sidewalk roller skates I had the measles. It was the three-day kind, but it ruined my holiday. I took the skates to bed with me and fantasized the hour that I could insert that key in the skates, tighten them on my shoe sole, and sail away." Her voice turns dreamy. "The following Christmas I broke my arm and spent half the winter in a plaster cast."

Every lady sitting at the table tsks in sympathy. How sad. What a shame. Terrible thing to happen on *Christmas.*

I join the conversation, reserving my resentment of Frances for later. "I only recall one Christmas. After dinner, our family prepared to listen to *The Life of Riley,* the *Red Skelton Show,* and the *Jack Benny Program* on the radio." My smile widens. "Mother popped corn, and since it was Saturday night, that meant it was hair-washing time, so after I shampooed, she rolled my long locks in pin curls. Dad sat in his big overstuffed chair and cracked walnuts, picking the meat out of the shell. Later Mother would make a batch of fudge — and I must say I have never been able to replicate her recipe. Her fudge was the best I've ever tasted."

Gwendolyn appears to do a mental tally. "Honey, you're not old enough to recall Jack Benny and *The Life of Riley.*"

"I'm not?"

Eleanor offers, "Perhaps you're remembering stories your parents told. Don't feel bad. That happens."

"My daughter gave me a set of *The Best of Jack Benny's Christmas Shows,* last year," Frances volunteers. "Want to come to my room and listen to them some night? Choose any night you want. I have nothing going on — except tonight. I have to work on the Christmas tree."

I find myself agreeing to the out-ing. By now I have forgotten why I was upset with Frances, and apparently I am missing a few years of Christmas memories.

Later, I stop by the birdcage to feed cracked eggshells to the little feathered creatures. I'm not sure when it happened, but someone put me in charge of feeding the birds that are kept in a big, floor-to-ceiling gilded cage near the main entryway. My job is to feed and water the birds once a day, but I throw in the eggshells because my grandmother kept birds and she fed them the treat. The chefs save the shells in a plastic bag and give them to me when I fold napkins with Gwendolyn in the morning.

"Hello, Henry." I kneel in front of

the cage and study the array of God's little creatures. I've given them all names. It only seems proper. Such trusting, carefree, and helpless creatures. Their tweets and twitters brighten the foyer, and the facility residents often spend hours sitting in the lobby, watching their activities. Yesterday I heard an older man quote what I believe was scripture. I heard him whisper, " 'Look at the birds of the air; they do not sow or reap or store away in barns, and yet your heavenly Father feeds them. Are you not much more valuable than they?' "

Often when I look in the mirror, I see a reflection and wonder if that person is valuable to God: a tiny, helpless creature with seemingly no purpose and yet I am fed and clothed and warm by no effort of my own.

I carefully distribute the crackly treat, and afterward I glance up and mentally gasp. At the end of corridor one, that man is busy at work at the outside entrance. He's peering over his shoulder like he's about to achieve a goal. I know that I should report him, but since I've already had one brush with Candace Marshall, administrator, today, I don't need a second one.

Fascinated, I watch him fiddle with something and then unhook a wire. With a final security glance, he quietly opens the door. No siren squeal. Nothing but normal sound fills the corridor.

I absently wipe my hands on my slacks and watch him slip through the doorway, envious of his success.

Dr. Important rounds the corner like a bat out of Hades and apparently spots the offense. His pace quickens. "Need help on corridor one!"

Shrugging my shoulders, I pick up the discarded napkin that contained the eggshells and continue to my room.

If one has to be busted, the infraction should be for something worthwhile, and for one precious moment the man has his freedom.

Chapter Eight

Year Four

December 12

A decorated blue spruce stands in the foyer, resplendent with silver tinsel and large white peacocks scattered among the spreading branches. Bing Crosby dreams of a white Christmas over the intercom. I add the finishing touches to my finger-painting project and shove the construction paper aside. "Where did you say Gerty is? I haven't seen her in days."

"She's sick, honey." The woman sitting across from me pushes back from the long worktable. Days blur slowly into one another. The craft room is near empty this morning, so I wander into the hallway and pause to speak to the first nurse that I spot. "Has Jack been in today?"

"No, Arlene. Not today, sweetie."

Time hangs heavy on my mind. Nobody's visited me for weeks. The only excitement in my life is meeting Una, who has fast become my dearest friend. Una's about my age. She stays to herself mostly and refuses to associate with the others, but we have developed a rather close relationship. To my delight, I learn that the newcomer and I share the same likes and dislikes. I can talk to her like a sister, tell her my deepest hurts and secrets, and she understands. She's the last person I speak to at night and usually the first I see in the morning.

And Una's even a Republican.

Dr. Important rushes past me on the way to the break room. I don't know if it's my imagination, but his hair looks darker these days. Una and I decide he's putting *color* on those graying locks.

Speaking of the doctor, Una asks me if I think that he is married. I say no. I don't know why, but I don't think many women would put up with him. I presume that he's quite an attractive man if he would slow down and let me get a better look, but I suspect it would take a strong woman to tame this male.

A couple of unfamiliar residents are sitting in the foyer playing solitaire. I don't enjoy the card game, but I decide to pull up a chair — at their invitation — and watch. Somebody mentions that a youth group from a local church is coming today to give manicures. One glance at my nails and I cringe. Where are the long, tapered gel nails with a tiny flower decal on the pointed tips? My gaze shifts to my dry skin that now looks like crepe paper. I abandon the inspection and stuff my hands beneath the folds of my sweater.

"Mom?"

I look up to see the woman that I now call "Melissa" standing in the foyer. Bits of snowflakes lie on her fur collar, and her blushed cheeks appear almost too red today. "Yes, dear?"

"Hi. I thought you might be in your room." Bracelets jingle and the scent of Elizabeth Taylor's Passion scents the foyer.

The solitaire ladies drop their cards and spring to their feet, cherry-color cheeks coming to life. "Why hello! Come in! Stay awhile," one invites.

I shoot out of my seat, grasping for Melissa's hand. She is *my* company. Not theirs. "She's here to visit *me.*" Peculiar how possessive the residents are. We act like selfish children when it comes to guests. We don't want to share.

Expectant smiles fade, and the women return to their hand of cards.

Melissa and I walk down the corridor, and I admire her fur-lined boots with a three-quarter heel. So trendy. Once I dressed like her . . . how long ago? I can't recall ever wearing anything but saggy pants and oversized blouses.

"Melissa?"

"Yes, Mom?"

"What happened to my leather jacket?"

"What jacket is that?"

"The one I was wearing in the crash. I'd just purchased it that day." The image is clear. I shopped my favorite store, and when I spotted the jacket, I cast prudence to the wind and paid the scandalous price for the garment.

Mention of the accident seems to unnerve the young lady. "I don't know. I imagine it was lost in the plane wreckage."

"Plane?"

Melissa tone softens. "You were in a plane crash."

"I was? Was I hurt?"

"You're doing very well."

"I really liked that jacket. I don't go out often," I confess, "but I'd like to have it." Gwendolyn wears her finest to meals. I might have the youth girls do my nails today, and then some night soon I will wear the jacket to dinner.

We enter my room, and I close the door. I don't want any snoop dogs sharing my guest.

Melissa peels out of her coat and lays the garment on the sofa. Today her pretty face is strained. Even weepy. Smudges of back mascara form around her eyelids.

"Are you feeling well, dear?"

Pulling me to the sofa, she eases me down. "Have you noticed that Jack hasn't been with me lately?"

"My Jack?"

"Jack Jr."

"Oh, him. No, I'm afraid that I haven't seen him in years."

"Mom, he visited you early this week. He — *we* want to come more often but by the time we fly here and back, the day is gone." Releasing a sigh, the woman bites her upper lip, and tears pool in her violet-colored eyes.

I immediately regret my careless observation. “Have I upset you?”

“It isn’t you. It’s me. I’m afraid that I’m about to upset you.” A ragged sob escapes her.

I like seeing her strong emotions. I can’t recall a time when anything upset me. I have no particular emotions. Confusion, but no deep-down responses. At the moment, I welcome a good righteous anger. Scooting forward, I say softly, “I may not understand your words, but I can listen.” I have the oddest feeling that she needs to talk to someone. Too bad it has to be me, but I’ll do what I can.

Hot tears roll from the young woman's eyelids. Such a pretty face to be so fragmented.

"What is it?"

"It's me . . . and Jack. We're separated."

I frown. "You and *my* Jack?" This explains why he hasn't been around to visit. My gaze skims the lovely creature with coal black hair that hangs below her collar and watery violet eyes. She is stunning. Young. Healthy. I glance at my worn hands and chipped nails. *Oh Jack. How could you?*

"Jack Jr., Mom."

My mood lifts. "He's my son."

"Yes, and my husband. We tried to save our marriage, but we'd drifted too far apart." She swipes at the wet stream trickling down her cheeks.

"Do you argue?"

"We barely say a civil word to each other." She looks at me and dabs at her nose. "I'm sorry — I know you can't understand, but I desperately need someone to talk to."

"Your mother?"

"She's in Europe for the holidays."

I sit back, wondering if I have been the sort of mother who would spend the holidays in Europe if my daughter needed me. "Go on. I'm listening."

"There's not much to tell. We've tried to keep our marriage from falling apart, but Jack works all the time and he says I'm too involved in my separate life." She shakes her head. "I live a separate life because I'm forced to — not because I want to. He's never around. Our home and social life has fallen apart."

Even I know that life has a way of separating couples who vow to love one another forever.

"Jack Jr. and I no longer have a private life. When we speak, we bark. The tension between us has grown until we can cut it with a knife. The last straw was when I forgot one of his clients was in town, and I was supposed to have taken her shopping. Instead, I went to Jazzercise." She drew a shuddering sigh. "He packed a bag and left that night."

I shake my head. "Seems a small thing to raise such a fuss over."

"That's what I said."

Images swim before me. I so need to help her, but all I can remember is the time a couple, both close friends of Jack and me, split up. "Jack and I had friends that indulged in the silliest disagreements. One time she wanted the garage door painted red, and her husband said he'd do it. She bought the paint, and he set to work on one of his rare days off. She was so busy that she let him do his thing. He poked his head in the doorway once and said, 'I think you'd better take a look at this.'

"My friend said, 'The color is fine, Jack. Just paint it.' It was one of her rare days off, too, and the man was capable of painting a garage door.

"Later when she wandered outside, she nearly dropped her coffee mug. The door was *pink.* Shocking, hideous pink. Was he color blind?

"He stopped work, and she drove back to the paint store. This time she returned with True Red. He set to work again. When she went out an hour later, she could not believe her eyes. The door was a cross between cranberry and dizzying red! She said that her dying geraniums were prettier.

"Her husband sat down on the driveway and took off his hat. The third bucket, she hit gold. Red Garnet, a lovely shade. When her husband completed the job, the door was perfect. She often asked me how many husbands would have painted that door three times in the same day."

I shrug. The conversation is as clear as a cloudless sky in my mind. "Of course, he didn't speak to her the rest of the night, but by morning, he was whistling while he dressed. Men recover quickly. That and she was wise enough to book a Caribbean cruise late that afternoon. She figured she owed her husband a little extra attention and appreciation."

"Oh Mom!" Melissa half laughs, half cries the exclamation. "Do you realize that you just spoke clear, long sentences? You *are* getting better!"

We both laugh. Seemed convoluted to me.

Wiping her eyes, Melissa dreams out loud. "I wish a Caribbean cruise would solve my problem."

By then I am back trying to figure out who I am speaking to. I know her — but I don't know her. "Well, who knows? It could."

It didn't take a full set of faculties to know that.

She shook her head. "I haven't spoken to or seen my Jack in weeks."

We sit in silence until I offer, "If he'd come to see me, I could speak to him about the matter."

"Mom, he comes to see you twice a month — and that's as often as he can. Steven and Julee are supposed to fill the void when we can't come."

"I never see Steven."

She leans to give me a hug. "I don't know why I'm bothering you. You can't do a thing about my problems. Are you okay?"

"How would I know? I can't remember squat — except an occasional flash. Sometimes at night when I'm lying in bed, I ask God, 'Why?' If I had to lose memory, why not make me like one sitting in the hallway, staring into thin air, without a care in the world. I recall just enough to aggravate me."

Melissa's gaze roams the room. "I know Jack and Steven spare no expense to keep you here, but are you comfortable?"

"What's not to be comfortable? I have everything but joy."

Scooting to the edge of the sofa, Melissa looks me in the eye, her gaze soft. "What would it take to restore your joy?"

"One thing. I want my Jack to come and see me. I miss him. It's been weeks since the accident, and I know he has to be back from that business trip by now."

Melissa falls silent, her gaze focused on the Persian rug beneath the coffee table. "Mom?"

"Yes?"

"Your Jack's been very ill."

Alarmed, I scoot to face her. "His heart?" Odd that I would recall his recent heart episode. I hadn't thought about it since the accident.

"Yes . . . his heart is involved."

Nausea wells to the back of my throat. "Is it serious?"

She takes both of my hands and holds them tightly. I detect a brief struggle in her eyes, and then strengthening her grasp, she says, "Jack would want me to remind you that whatever happens in this life, you and he will be reunited in heaven."

I latch onto her arm. "Melissa. You can tell me the truth. Is Jack alive?" From day one I have refused to consider the possibility that Jack might no longer be with me, but time passes, and it gets harder to shove the unthinkable aside.

Her lovely gaze focuses on me.

Tender. Caring. "He's even better than that, Mom. He's somewhere where he'll never grow old and his heart will never give out."

Flashes of a young, bearded man wearing a white robe and sandals rush to mind. His eyes are tender, and He is holding a small child on His lap. "Heaven?" I venture.

"Yes, I truly believe he is there, Mom."

My hand drops away, and I sit back with an almost giddy feeling. Jack isn't ignoring me; he has been too ill to visit. His heart needed more than a stent. "I wish I could have said good-bye."

Kiss him one final time. Feel his strength in my weakness.

"He would have liked that, Mom.

You know you and Dad had an enviable marriage. You truly loved each other."

I glance up. "Thank you for telling me, Melissa. You don't know how many nights I've lain awake wondering about Jack. Is he traveling? Is he eating well? I never once considered his heart."

"I know, Mom. I have seen your concern, but I believe that you sense that life is unpredictable. Tomorrow you won't recall this conversation, but when you ask Jack Jr. or Steven about their father, Jack Jr. will remind you that your Jack is in heaven now."

Nodding, I say, "I'll try." For the first time in a long time, I am aware of hot salty tears streaming down my cheeks, filling my nose. For a second, I can't breathe. My Jack is gone. I reach for a tissue.

After a bit, I wipe my eyes and say, "I would like for you to come more often, Melissa. Perhaps we can help each other."

"Maybe we can, Mom." She lightly blows her nose and then draws in a long sigh. "You're so young to be here — in this place."

Gwendolyn, Eleanor, Frances — and almost anyone I can name — are older than me. Only Una looks to be near my age.

"Have I told you about my friend Una?"

"You have. Perhaps we can have lunch together very soon."

"I don't know." I think about it.

"Una doesn't like most of the people in here. She stays to herself a lot. She's going home soon."

"I'm sorry. Perhaps one day we'll go to her room and meet with her in private."

"Okay. I can convince her to meet you. She always asks about my family."

"Maybe the next visit?"

"Sure." I'm not going anywhere.

Chapter Nine

Year Five

October 31

Children's laughter fills the corridors. Squeals and fussy cries burst forth from sticky faces with even stickier hands.

I sit on the stool, wearing the Cinderella costume and hand out candy. There were shouts of protests and some pretty unfriendly looks when the prize dress landed in my hands. I don't know why. I can't ever recall wearing the garment.

One lady accused me of cheating — me, Arlene Santana, who once went out of her way to return change when a cashier overpaid me. Then again, maybe I only imagine what I'm like. The thought does occupy time. Am I a fussy person? Rude? Or rather am I the sort everybody likes? I prefer the latter.

Gwendolyn overheard the snide accusation and flew into the loudmouth know-it-all like a chicken on a June bug. That's Gwendolyn, always protecting me. Yet often her and Frances's feistiness lands me in trouble. Una says I should stay clear of my tablemates; they're troublemakers.

And to my shame, I walked away

with the Cinderella dress this morning feeling a bit superior.

Little guys draw back when I offer their treat, eyes round with wonder. I hand out candy as quick as my hand can keep up when I glance up to see Steven and Julee coming through the line, carrying a little blond-haired, blue-eyed girl. I've never seen the child before, but she is something special. Just the sight of her makes my heart happy. The child's features are purely angelic and turn my heart to soup.

"Why, Steven! What a surprise to see you!" I bound off my throne — actually a bar stool draped in a sheet that the janitor has fashioned — and hug the man so tightly he staggers backward. "It is so good to see you!" I affectionately punch his shoulder. "Where have you two been? And Jack Jr., is he with you?"

"No, it's just us tonight, Mom."

"My Jack is gone," I say. "He's waiting somewhere for me. Can you take me there?"

Steven straightens, holding tight to the little girl now. On closer inspection I see the priceless child isn't so small. She must be four or five years old. "Look, Mom. I've brought someone to visit you."

My gaze skims the beautiful child dressed in Tinker Bell green, her tiny shoes, a wand clutched in her slightly chubby fist. I reach and tenderly adjust the tilted crown sitting atop her golden hair. "What an angel. Who is she?"

"This is Ella, Mom."

"Ella." I stand and admire God's perfect work. "I have a granddaughter. Ella Parker." I glance up and smile. "She must be four or five months old now. Did I mention that's where your father and I were going when we had the . . . train wreck?"

I swallow back a lump with the fresh reminder of Jack. Each time I think of the senseless loss, I break into tears. "Steven, where is —" I catch back my question. I promised someone that I wouldn't ask about Jack anymore. Somehow, deep down where it counts, I know that he is somewhere safe, unaffected by the accident, and I no longer worry so much about him. I will see him soon.

"Ella, can you give Grandma Arlene a big hug?" Julee urges the child's affection. The little girl obediently bends down from Steven's arms, and a noisy smack lands on my cheek.

"Oh my!" I fondly touch the icky substance clinging to my face. Chocolate? Tootsie Pop. "What a lovely kiss — why, I believe such affection deserves *two* pieces of candy." I drop the additional treat in the child's bucket.

The line is backing up, and Steven and Julee are forced to move along. My gaze follows the little girl until her parents round the corner and I can no longer see her. My cheek feels faintly warm from gluey lips.

Everyone's in such a hurry these days. Smiles come and go, coloring my life briefly, but when I climb in bed after a "family event," I feel empty.

I remind myself that my family sees me when they can; I can't be selfish. But days — and nights — here can be very long.

You can imagine my surprise when I return to my room later and Steven is waiting there, sitting on my sofa. My eyes search for the little girl.

"It's way past Ella's bedtime," he says. "Julee took her home and put her to bed."

"I'm so glad that you stayed, Steven." I sit down opposite him, feeling a bit foolish in my Cinderella costume. The garb suits my peculiar life perfectly. Everyone here seems to be seeking carefree, youthful days and to do and say things they wouldn't have thought to do or say in earlier years. Like dress as Cinderella and Little Bo Peep.

"The little girl is lovely. I hope you'll bring her again soon."

We chat for a few minutes, and I focus on the tight lines around my boy's eyes. Jack calls those "responsibility lines." I ease to the front of my chair. "Is everything okay with you, Steven?" *Steven is my quiet child.* The thought just pops into my mind. Jack Jr. can talk a leg off a chair, but Steven rarely does or says anything without purpose.

"There's something worrying you, isn't there?"

Call it motherly instinct — though I am a pitiful shell of a mother — but I know something is amiss. The unspoken guilt in his eyes reminds me of when I had been a much better parent. "What is it, darling?"

He squirms and leaves the sofa. Stuffing his hands in his trouser pockets, he walks to the window. "I've done something that I don't want Julee to know about."

Some persistent devil tears at him; I can see anxiety in his expression. It's the same look he had on his face when he broke his arm and two ribs in a motorbike accident. Scraped, bloody, bruised arms wound around my neck after Jack and I burst into the emergency room and rushed to the gurney.

"Go on."

He swallows, his Adam's apple working in his throat. "I've wanted to buy a new motorcycle for some time now."

That doesn't sound like the end of the world. "Julee doesn't like motorcycles?" I'm grasping now. Maybe if he'd get to the point I could help. I'd never encouraged the machine.

Shaking his head negatively, he says softly, "I don't know why I'm bothering you with this; you won't remember our conversation tomorrow, but I need your wisdom tonight, Mom. I'm scared to death." He turns from the window to meet my gaze. "She's going to kill me."

I think about the response and gather he's exaggerating. Julee doesn't seem the violent sort.

Opening my arms wide, I offer what little I can because I know that my baby is scared — or hurt — and I won't kill him. The thought is so gratifying after endless weeks of confusion and uncertainty. Tonight I am Momma again. Steven steps into my arms, and I just hold him. Once I held a fragile child; tonight I hold a man. Is he a good man? Kind? Dedicated to his wife and family?

"Everything will be fine," I say, giving what I assume is a mother's expected reply. I know nothing about his angst, and I'm aware that

I am his mother only in heart. But for this precious moment, I throw everything left of Arlene Santana — which isn't a lot — into comforting my boy.

"Why are you so worried, Steven?"

"Mom, I don't know what happened. I was in the motorcycle shop today — and before I knew it, I bought another machine."

"And Julee doesn't like motorcycles. I recall those dangerous, deafening things."

"She's okay with them, and we've talked about me buying a new bike, but Julee thinks it's a waste of money. She reminds me that I don't have time to ride the one I have and we don't need another one sitting in the garage. But today I was in the bike shop, and I saw this one — Mom, you'd have to see it to appreciate it. Before I knew it, I'd bought it." He turns sad eyes my way. "I have to tell her when I get home."

"Oh my." I can't help him. God might.

"She's going to kill me."

I spring to my feet. "Is it a matter of money? I think I might have some tucked away — though I'll have to ask Jack Jr." Jack Jr. said to tell him if I need anything.

"It isn't money, Mom. Julee told me a month ago if I brought another motorcycle home she'd divorce me."

"Really?" I give that some serious

thought, not fully understanding the conversation but willing to find a solution. I dig deep in the recess of my mind.

Reason it out, Arlene. If a person has money, but his wife doesn't want him to spend it . . .

"She's going to be upset. She's wanted to remodel an upstairs bathroom, and you know how frugal she is with money."

I spring to my feet. "Return the motorcycle to the store."

His expression turns dark. "I don't want to return it; it's a SuperLow 1200, Harley."

"But if you have another one —"

"Not like this one."

"Well, then." I sit back down to ponder the dilemma. "I suppose you'll just have to put your foot down." That's Jack's answer to any problem. *"Just put your foot down, Arlene."* I sit a moment longer and then casually slip my foot over his.

He focuses on the tip of my shoe on top of his boot. "What are you doing, Mom?"

"Putting my foot down — that's what I need to do." Though honestly, I can't see a bit of sense in taking this approach. What possible difference can it make if Steven smashes Julee's foot? The response will only further infuriate her.

We talk a few moments longer, but then he says that's he's spent a long day wiring something. Finally he says good night, and I rise to walk him to the entrance, sensing that the last thing my son wants is to face an irate wife.

Faintly lit corridors are empty when we step from my room. No trace remains of tiny tots with sticky hands and impatient cries other than an occasional bright yellow discarded M&M's bag. I walk beside Steven, gripping his hand as though we are about to enter a crosswalk. Or is he holding my hand to prevent a fall? I don't walk as even as I once did.

When we round the corner, I notice Dr. Important leaning against the reception desk, studying a chart. Shiny brown loafers glisten with a coat of wax, and a hint of brown sock peeks above the sides. The two solitaire players are at their usual observation post. When Steven walks by, I nudge him closer to the center of the hallway, giving the women a warning look. Busybodies always trying to butt in on other people's company.

Nodding coolly, I accompany my handsome guest to the front door.

"Tell Jack Jr. and Melissa that I would like to see them soon." I button the top button on Steven's leather jacket. He's inherited his daddy's good looks, streaked blond hair, and blue eyes.

"Thanks, Mom." He bends to kiss my cheek and then exits, walking to his truck, shoulders bent.

I feel bad for him. Common sense tells me that Julee is still going to make him take the bike back.

I'm practically bowled over when the two front-entrance doors fly open and a young, harried man bursts inside. "My wife's having a baby in the cab!"

The chart flies in the air, and Dr. Important grabs a gurney. "This isn't a hospital!" he calls.

"We don't have time for a hospital. Quick! She's about to have my boy!"

I right myself as the doctor shoves the stretcher through the open doorway.

Shortly afterward, the entrance doors fly open, and in walks a woman madder than a wet hen. Fury mars her face. She clutches her unbuttoned skirt tightly to her waist. "I *never*!"

"Ma'am." Dr. Important trails her in, his eyes as round as cup saucers. "I swear I would have *never* ripped your skirt off if I had known!"

"What kind of *doctor* are you?" she screeches. "I am going to report this — this travesty!"

"Ma'am." Doctor glances at the gathering crowd. "I . . . he said . . . in the cab . . . baby coming!"

"There are *two* cabs sitting at the curb, jerk! Are you blind?"

I, though naughty, can't help but snicker. Dr. Important is still trying to explain his rash actions as he trails the aggravated woman down the hallway.

See Arlene, some days it does pay to get out of bed.

CHAPTER TEN

Every now and then, something agreeable happens in Sunset Gardens of Buckhead. Some little ditty comes along that starts the day off with a smile.

Una spends nearly the whole day with me. Our visits are what keep me going. Few around me know their names or the time of day — not to mention proper etiquette — but Una knows everything. Etiquette. Manners. Knowledge of foreign countries. She must be well traveled. And goodness knows that I'm not looking forward to one more egg or dry piece of toast, so her longer-than-usual visit this morning is welcomed with open arms.

Una and I talk about our problems, and I realize again why I like this woman so much. We have nearly everything in common. She likes solitude; I like solitude. She thinks the facility where we're expected to call "home" is nice but much prefers her lovely home where everything has its place. In this place, we agree, we can't find a blessed thing. Laundry gets mixed up, personal items disappear, and I don't know how long it's been since I've seen my pair of comfortable white sneakers.

We visit so long today that I'm late for breakfast, but this morning I can talk of nothing else but my new friend.

"Is she a saint or something?" Eleanor asks. My tablemates have dwindled. Gwen's caught a bug, and Frances's chair is vacant. She must be skipping meals again. Ninety-some-odd years, and the little lady still fights on to maintain her trim waistline. Me? I would give up and order a second dessert.

"I don't know how long Una's been here, but you would like her. She's interesting and makes me laugh a lot."

Amusement is often hard to find in this place. I overhear two nurses talking about wishes. I had forgotten the word exists. If I had two wishes, I would only use one. Home. I wish I could go home and leave this monkey cage, but that's never going to happen. I will be rolled out on that stretcher Gwendolyn mentioned the first morning we met.

I finish my toast and pat my lips with a napkin. "Una and I are going to be friends forever."

Eleanor spills her coffee, and her sleeve drags through the mess as she reaches for a clean napkin. I have taken her to task about the worrisome habit, but she doesn't listen. "Why not invite her to sit at our table? Tell her she can — we can make room."

"Una takes her meals in her room." With a mental sigh, I wish it wasn't so; she would be a welcome addition to mealtimes. On the other hand, I think a small part of me doesn't want to share her with my other friends.

Excusing myself, I leave the table and wave down a worker.

"I'll take Gwendolyn's breakfast to her on a tray this morning."

The smiling woman brushes the offer aside. "We'll do that, Mrs. Santana."

I straighten, pulling to my full height. "If you don't mind, I'll do it." Rarely do I talk back, but if I don't feed Gwen, what else would I do this early? I've fed the birds, and toilet-roll art doesn't start for two hours.

Shrugging, the nurse walks away, and I take the gesture to mean that she doesn't have time to argue.

Gwendolyn is still in bed when I elbow the door to her room open. The interior is dark as pitch. Stale air meets my nose. Something on the bed stirs. "Who is it?"

"Good morning, dear, I brought your breakfast." When I told the chief cook what I needed, he stopped long enough to assemble a breakfast plate. I picked up a small vase with a plastic blue flower on my way out of the dining room and set it on the tray.

Struggling to open her eyes, Gwendolyn mumbles, "I don't have an appetite this morning."

"Oh, sure you do." I set the tray on the table and help her find the remote that raises and lowers her bed. Giving it a punch, I watch Gwendolyn's body go up, up, up until she says, "Whoa. You trying to break me in two?"

I proceed to straighten her tumbled sheets and light blanket. To me, the cover is too thin. "Did you get cold last night?" The wind blew and rattled windows till dawn.

"Yes, so cold. I punched my light, but nobody came. So I yelled for someone to bring me an extra blanket, but nobody came."

Hiding a smile, I sympathize, but I know from experience that Gwendolyn is a yeller. She yells for everything, day and night, and one would be hard pressed to know if her problem needs immediate attention. "Perhaps it only seemed like hours."

The staff is overwhelmed at times. Lights glow over doorways; bells go off at the nurse's station. It doesn't matter if it's light or dark, the staff operates at a dead run.

I move the bedside tray closer and lift the stainless steel cover. A poached egg meets my inspection. Dry toast, a bowl of Cheerios, orange juice, and a pot of hot water for tea.

Gwendolyn is on corridor three, and the dining room sits near the front entrance, so it took me awhile to deliver the heavy tray. The egg has to be stone-cold. Gwendolyn's skeptical eyes sweep the offering, which makes me think that she fears the same. "I'll just have tea and whatever's in that bowl."

I carefully tuck a napkin beneath her chin and set the cold egg aside. "Maybe you'll feel more like eating at lunch."

"I doubt it."

Arranging her tray for more suitable access, I ask, "Can I keep you company while you eat?"

I can always go to the small sunroom in corridor one and listen to Doreen Masters play the organ. She isn't bad — but in my limited understanding, I suspect she isn't good either.

Gwendolyn fumbles, knocks over the glass of orange juice, and spills a couple of packets of artificial sweetener before she manages to pour enough hot water in her cup to make tea. Her hand trembles as though she's shaking salt on watermelon.

Old age is brutal.

By the time I manage to change Gwendolyn's gown, her tea is cold, and we have to start over. I make the trek to the kitchen for more hot water and return as Gwendolyn concentrates on her bowl of Cheerios.

Lifting her spoon, she mechanically scoops the little round Os into her mouth, catching a stray piece with the tip of her tongue. Her tray looks like a bomb has exploded. Cup overturned, eating utensils poked in food. I spot a piece of toast between her sheets as I fix her cup of tea.

"Well" — I sit down and cross my hands — "I guess the holidays are coming up."

I've stopped counting Christmases. There have been so many, and the way time passes makes my head swim.

"Yes, suppose they are." Gwendolyn's hand pauses in midair. "Never cared for this time of the year."

Frowning, I lean closer.

"My deceased husband, Pete, was a no-good, and what brings excitement to most brings dread to me. Even my youthful memories are those of hard work and little to eat."

I listen, shaking my head. The holidays are joyfully celebrated in my home. Baking, hanging wreaths, wrapping presents in the basement until early dawn. "Jack and I rarely lift our voices to one another, though we often have sharp differences."

Gwen spoons whole wheat Os into her mouth. "Heard Orville Myers took off his number-two diaper and hurled it at his nurse last night. No call for such ugliness."

I have to work to keep up with the abrupt change of subject. What does Orville and dirty diapers have to do with wrapping presents? "No, I haven't heard. He's a cranky old man."

Pausing, Gwendolyn lifts a spoonful of cereal and studies it. "I'll never understand why they feed us butter beans for breakfast."

I ease to the edge of my chair, peering at the fare. "Butter beans?"

"Butter beans. See?" Gwendolyn's eyes motion to the spoon. "Butter beans. Have you ever seen the likes?"

Guest activity is picking up. There are more visitors coming and going, bringing potted plants to residents. When I return from my daily walk, I note with surprise that I have company. Jack Jr. and Melissa wait in my room. The woman is arranging a small bouquet of cut flowers in the vase beside my bed. I pause in the doorway, taken aback by the sight. Organ music swells from corridor one.

Jack Jr. flashes a grin that reminds me so much of Jack Sr. that my heart nearly stops. "There you are, Mom."

"Why — my!" I clasp my hands to my chest. I have spent eyes from studying my family pictures, and I feel rather good the effort has paid off. I can almost with certainty identify Jack Jr., Steven, and the two ladies they bring with them. Melissa and Julee. "Is it a holiday again? I wondered why the corridors smell so festive today."

The man crosses the room to give me a bear hug. "Sorry we haven't been to see you lately. I've had a big case, and Missy's . . . always tied up."

I know. He doesn't have to explain; the time it takes to excuse why he doesn't visit cuts into today's visit. They never stay long, anyway. There is something I need to speak to him about. My eyes move from the pretty lady — *Melissa,* I remind myself of her name — to the man, Jack Jr. Something very important that I need to tell him, but I can't recall what.

"You know who I am, don't you, Mom?"

"Why, silly. Of course I know who you are." I enter the room and store the cane that I'm carrying these days. Does he think I'm feeble? "I hoped you'd come today." My eyes automatically skim the room in search of Jack Sr., but I don't mention my husband's name. The subject only upsets the couple.

The woman steps around him, smiling. "Come see what I've brought you, Arlene." She turns me toward the bed and points to the lovely bouquet of fresh-cut flowers and a pink nightgown. Both are nice. Her perfume is even lovelier. Elizabeth Taylor's Passion.

"Now don't ask, 'What am I going to do with the gown?' You'll wear it," the man says.

His voice is patient — almost patronizing. I do not appreciate the work-with-me tone. I ease closer, my eyes assessing him, feeling a bit daring. "Where am I going to wear it?" The garment is beautiful but completely out of place in the dining room, and I will freeze sleeping in the sheer fabric.

He guides me over to the straight-back chair and sits me down. He perches on the sofa. "What have you been up to these days?"

I need a moment to sort through my answer. Each day is the same. "Did I tell you that I got the place of honor at the door this Halloween?"

"Congratulations." He addresses the woman in a cool tone. "Steve brought Ella by this year, didn't he?"

"Of course he did, Jack." Her tone is cordial but guarded.

I change subjects because it seems

to me that these two have a gate between them — a big iron gate that prevents them for speaking in cordial tones. "Have I told you about my best friend, Una? We have grown so close. I feel like she's family."

He nods, smiling. So like my husband, Jack. "I'm glad that you have a special friend."

"It's the best friendship ever," I admit. "I don't know how I'd pass the time without our long talks."

"Some night," the man promises, "I am going to come and have dinner with you and Una. Would you like that?"

"I would love that." I smile at the pretty woman, who is busy tucking the new nightgown in the drawer.

"Miss . . ." Her name is on the tip of my tongue but won't slide out. "I want you to come, too." The facility has a special room — a separate area where people who love each other gather to eat. I never personally get to use the room, but I see and hear the contagious laughter coming from behind closed double doors.

The man nods. "It's a date. Make a note of the day on that oh-so-important calendar, Melissa. It's high time that we meet Una." He gives my hand a firm squeeze.

"I'll do that, Jack — and you make certain to leave ten minutes open so that you can join us. I'm sure the country club and your golf buddies will understand." She bends forward to quietly speak to me. "Thank you, Arlene, I'd love to have dinner with you and Una."

I stare at her. "Gwendolyn thought she was eating butter beans for breakfast. Isn't that funny?" There are so few comical events around here; the mistake suddenly strikes me as hilarious.

The lady's gaze slides to the man's, and a hesitant smile parts ruby-red lips. "Charming."

"She was eating Cheerios," I clarify.

"Oh." She sends another brief glancing smile toward the man. "How very . . . witty."

I don't think Gwen was trying to be witty; she really thought she was eating beans.

The man's name rushes back, and I make sure to use it. "Jack Jr.?"

"Yes, Mom?"

"Is that a bit of silver I see in your hair?"

He runs a self-conscious hand over the top of his head. "My barber must have missed a patch."

"Silver is attractive. My Jack was gray by the time he was thirty." I can remember almost everything about my husband — his grin, his flirty looks, his teasing remarks — yet I don't recall when or how I met him or married him. Memories flicker and evaporate into thin air.

"Mom." Jack Jr.'s features sober. "Are you happy here?"

"Happy?" The answer surfaces like a fishing bobber. "I don't think so, dear."

"Would you like to move to another facility? Can we do anything to make this time in your life easier?"

Such a serious George. He sounds like he's wrecked his new bicycle and dreads to tell me. "I don't think so. I don't want to be a bother."

"Melissa" — his gaze switches to the woman — "feels that you would be happier elsewhere. You have everything you need, don't you, Mom? If you want anything, you know that all you have to do is pick up the phone." He pauses. "Have one of the staff call me or Steven. We haven't left you here to . . ." Clearing his throat, he starts again.

"Steven and Julee are fifteen minutes from here. If you ever need or want us for anything, all you have to do is let them know."

"Really?" I think about his generous offer. Dare I tell him that I live to go home to my bed, my cozy electric blanket? Drift off to sleep with the sound of my creaky old furnace coming on and off and the big old house settling down for a long winter night?

"Mom?"

I look up. "Did I mention that Milton Ashley on corridor four was caught sneaking into a woman's room after hours?"

Considering their vacant stares, I must not have mentioned the incident. So I tell them. "The occasion created quite a stink. Even the chefs make innuendoes about ol' Milt when Frances and I fold napkins. Milton's actions are disgraceful: That's what Frances says. He should be banned from the general population. A man his age needs to stuff his hands in his pocket and avoid temptation.

"I sidestep men," I assure my guests, thinking out loud now. "I'm a married woman." It's not that Milt hasn't tried to catch my eye, but I am not interested in such nonsense. My Jack will put that man in his proper place when he hears about the flirting.

The visit lasts a few sentences longer. Enjoyable, cordial, even loving, but I sense a great deal of tension between the couple.

"What do you want for Christmas?" Jack asks when he slips into his tan overcoat.

What do I want for Christmas? Haven't they just brought me flowers and a new gown? My mind is blank. I have a bed, a closet, and a chair. A bed tray. Tall windows and fancy drapes.

Maybe stamps. Everyone in the facility has their own stamps. I don't know of a soul to write to, but I probably need stamps.

"How about clothing?" Missy offers. "Perhaps a new dress — shoes?"

"No," I refuse politely. I have a closet full of pants that hang like gunnysacks on me, and the blouses stretch across my bosom like shrink wrap. The last thing I need is more clothing that doesn't fit.

"Just stamps," I say and know in my heart I will get another pair of saggy slacks. Heavenly baking scents drift from the hallway. It surely must be a special day. "Are you going to stay and eat dinner with me?" If I had known they were coming I could have reserved the special room.

"Can't today, Mom." He lifts his shirt cuff and consults his fancy gold watch. "Wow. Look at the time. I have to be going."

"So good to see you, Mom." The woman gives me a little hug. "You have a wonderful dinner with your tablemates."

"Gwendolyn's sick. She won't be at the table."

The man appears surprised. "Wasn't she sick this time last year? What a shame."

"But there'll be others at your table, won't there?" Missy adds.

Now they are confusing me. The woman's prompting smile makes me sorry I've hinted at disappointment. There are others, the same old tired faces that I see day in and day out. I latch onto the woman's coattail. "You will come back and have dinner with me some night? Meet Una?"

"Of course we will." She pats my hand. "Soon, I promise. And tell Una hello for us. We can't wait to meet her."

The man bends and gives me a kiss that leaves my cheek smelling like a brisk autumn rain shower. "Take care of yourself, Mom." His voice lowers. "I love you — you know that, don't you?"

"I love you, too." I want to add his name. I had it a minute ago, but it's slipped out of reach again.

The woman reaches for the big red satchel. Long, bright red nails flash. I walk the couple to the doorway and eye the woman sideways, longing to ask about my Jack but sensing the subject is off limits.

"You have a good day." The man gives me one last peck on the temple, and I stand in the doorway, the smell of his aftershave fading as I watch the couple walk down the hallway, greeting staff. In many ways they remind me of Jack and me in earlier days. Happy. Confident. So very busy and important.

But so very cold to each another. That wasn't Jack's way or mine.

I turn and walk back to my bed and sit down, staring at my hands. There's a lovely diamond, not overly large, on the third finger of my right hand. It's very pretty, but the hands aren't my hands. These are old hands. Red and dry. I have lotion in my bedside table but forget to apply it. Someone comes to polish nails weekly — one young woman or another who chews bubble gum and giggles a lot. The effort is appreciated. They try, but often the polish globs in the corner of my nails.

A sigh catches in my throat. I'm sure that if Melissa is bent on buying me clothing, she will at least try to find something that fits.

Suddenly I sit straight up. bareMinerals. *That's* what I want for Christmas.

Drat. Getting out of bed, I scribble a note: *bareMinerals. Melissa.*

Climbing beneath the covers, I relax, glad to have that over.

Thank goodness makeup doesn't come in sizes.

Chapter Eleven

"Coffee, Arlene?"

I turn when the stout, friendly lady holding a coffeepot breaks into my woolgathering. "I believe I'll have tea this morning, thank you."

"I'll get that right away." The lady smiles and moves on to pour her offering to a couple, who nod and greet her with wavering smiles. There aren't many smiles in this place. Pitiful few are firm and confident; most are mere wisps, hesitant and given like money from a stingy banker.

After a while, I amble to my table. Unfolding my napkin, I am reminded that it will be awhile before my dining companions join me. Even as the thought passes through my mind, Gwendolyn shows up, looking a bit shaky on her feet. The back of her silver hair has a large pillow crease, and my hand automatically comes up to check my appearance. She makes a big deal of seating herself, scraping chair legs, rattling glasses.

"Well," she notes, her eyes pinpointing me. "Are you going to ask how I'm feeling?"

My mind might as well be a blank sheet of paper. "Should I?"

"I've been sick again." She jerks

the chair free of the table and lowers her bulk into it.

"You have?" Well, now I feel awful. I should have visited her. I have nothing else to do. Images of birds and snow-white napkins come to mind but make no sense. I don't know what I do with my time. "I'm sorry."

She stares at me and shakes her head. I hope she isn't going to remind me that I can't remember squat. I'm getting a little tired of that allegation. "I hope you're feeling better?"

Her striking blue eyes have yet to regain their earlier fiery intensity, but her tongue can still pierce marble when she wants, and if she isn't reprimanding she can break out in tears and give a warm hug. Unlike Frances, who has fangs and bites and doesn't care who gets bitten. The former librarian is English. Stiff upper lip, she likes to remind when anyone at the table complains about a minor ache or pain. "Life isn't a carousel in an amusement park," she repeats.

As if our dreary group isn't reminder enough.

Eleanor is ninety-one and the oldest of the group. She rarely contributes to conversations. The occasional nod or poke if she wants more butter covers her requests. When she does speak, her voice is so low I have to bend to catch her words.

Gwendolyn's voice, on the other

hand, ricochets like heavy thunder and slices through the drapes, blathering on and on about her knitting, the sheer brilliance of great-grandchildren, her seven daughters who never come to see her, and a no-good, cheating husband who had taken their prize horse and left her twenty-seven years ago, shortly after her last child's birth, for a woman half his age.

Her blue eyes narrow, and I can hear her teeth grind. "I still miss that horse."

I am halfway through my cup of tea when Eleanor arrives, cheerful as a songbird this morning. "Just got the word," she says in low tones, "the Christmas tree is going up today." She hooks her cane over the back of her chair and sits down. "Have you been asked to help?"

"It's *Christmas* again?" I shake my head. It seems I've decorated that tree fifty times since I've been here.

Frances joins us and shoves her empty coffee cup to the side. "My stomach won't tolerate mud this morning. I want citrus tea."

Ha, I think. *Citrus tea. Here?* But moments later, a lady is holding a box open for Frances's inspection. The librarian smugly glances my way and plucks a bag from the box.

Shaking my head, I admit that I don't recall being asked to help decorate the tree.

"Shame." Eleanor opens her napkin and creases it flat in her lap. "There's so little enjoyment around here." Her faded brown eyes graze the filling dining room. "A few get to do everything special, but occasionally — if you're standing up there when the tree goes up — you can help."

Vermont was never lovelier than during the Christmas season.

I glance out the window and wonder why the weather is so different here. Mild . . . bordering on blistering, at times. I haven't witnessed a large snow in . . . well, I couldn't recall the last time.

"Do you ever wonder why it doesn't snow?"

"In Georgia?" Frances spoons oatmeal into her mouth. "You're plain off your rocker, lady."

"Georgia?"

"You're in Atlanta, Georgia, girl. Been here for what — more than four years? We can get some big snows, but it's rare; nothing like where you're from."

Anger flares. I'm not the irritable sort, not like some around here, but the idea that Frances would deceive me and tell me that I am in *Georgia* floors me. Has the woman lost *her* mind?

Eleanor lays her spoon down. "Well, look who's crabby."

Clamping my mouth shut, I sit back and refuse to finish my tea.

Frances motions toward the butter dish. When I pass the item, I ask, "Do you *work* today?" I have my disagreeable side, too.

Eleanor laughs, catching a speck of toast that flies from her mouth.

Word around the facility is Frances is making a big pest of herself, going to "work" in the office every day. She's a plain nuisance, I hear. The nurses cannot get her to understand that she doesn't work there and she's under no requirement to show up bright and early every morning. This has been going on for a month.

"None of *your* beeswax." The librarian's chin juts out like a billy goat.

I decide to keep quiet and just sit here and make both tablemates feel uncomfortable.

Eleanor doesn't notice the sudden chill and chats away. Blah de-blah, de-blah. Someone please hand me a rope so I can hang myself.

Finally the meal is over, and I head for my room. Una will be there by now, and we can have a civil conversation. Before I reach my destination, I spot the nurse's cart, hoping the torturer won't see me. But she glances up, motioning me over. I automatically slide the sleeve of my blouse past my elbow.

If they don't want me to eat pie, why do they offer it?

A soft prick and then, "There you go, sweetie." The nurse smiles and disposes of the paraphernalia.

The words are on the tip of my tongue to ask why I am singled out to be poked, but I've learned, don't ask why. Just accept.

By the time dinner rolls around, Frances is singing a different tune. I'd almost decided to confront her over her outrageous and delusional statement that I am in Georgia when I spot her at her self-appointed "work" station. I pause to watch the fiasco.

A nurse kneels in a pile of folders spilled to the floor. I look closer. Are those tears in the RN's eyes? Frances stands over her, peering through thick, horn-rimmed glasses. "Did I do that?" She snags a tissue and hands it to the nurse.

"It's fine . . . Frances." Sucking in air, the nurse gets to her feet with an armful of folders stacked to her chin.

"Think I'll tackle those medical charts now." Frances turns when the nurse drops the stack of folders.

Frances's drawn-on brows narrow. "It's going to take all day tomorrow to sort those out, you know."

"Frances dear." The nurse takes her by the arm and sits her down at the desk. I ease closer, not wanting to miss a word of this. "In my line of work, I am called upon to do many unpleasant tasks."

Frances nods. "Me, too." She glances at the pile of papers. "Like sort those."

The RN continues. "The hardest

is to tell someone that because of unforeseen circumstances, the facility — especially the staff — must downsize."

Nodding, Frances listens.

"Do you understand what I'm saying?"

Nodding, Frances smiles. "I'm getting fired."

"No. Laid off."

"Not fired."

"No, not fired, but you aren't to come to work until I send word that the budget cuts are over and we are free to resume a full office staff."

"Okay." Frances's gaze roams the work area. "I'm getting a little worn out from getting up so early."

"You can sleep in now." The nurse

gives her a gentle pat. "All day, if you want."

"Okay." Frances picks up her purse and hooks the strap over her arm. "I'll wait in my room until you send for me."

"Yes — thank you. You don't have to remain in your room; just don't come to work mornings."

"What about my Christmas bonus?"

By now the nurse is shuffling folders. "I'll have it delivered to your room."

"Okay. Merry Christmas."

"Same to you."

Chapter Twelve

Jack Jr. and Missy rarely come at the same time anymore. The thought strikes me Sunday afternoon, late in the day. Tension between the couple is noticeable, even to me. Snappish answers directed at each other, no eye-to-eye contact. I'd say there is trouble brewing, but then what do I know?

Holiday festivities brighten my spirit, and I think I've caught a little of the Christmas spirit going around. I begin to worry about gifts. Seems everyone is talking about what to get someone for Christmas. I know nothing about my children's lives now. Steven and Julee and the little blond-headed girl come. We have a good time, and I treasure the moments that I spend with little Ella, but I want to see my Ella. My goodness, at the rate I'm going, my grandchild will be potty trained before I meet her. Not really, but she must be getting close to nine months old. Why doesn't someone bring her to meet me?

Rays of late-afternoon sunshine dance on my carpet when Jack and Melissa settle on my sofa. "Well, this is nice," I say. "I haven't seen the two of you together in a while, have I?"

Jack avoids the woman's eyes. "It's a busy world, Mom."

"I know, but never too busy to stop and take the time to love one another."

Melissa's gaze shifts to the watercolor landscape above my head.

"You know, Jack." I slide to the edge of my chair and take his hand. I rarely initiate touch. Nobody "feels" right. But today I'm braver. "I once knew a couple who had a blessed marriage. Their friends — every last one of them — wanted to know their secret. And they had one."

Melissa's gaze shifts back to me.

"The woman confided to me that the marriage had not always been good. They encountered their fair share of . . ." I search for the word.

"Marital problems?" Melissa supplies.

"I believe that is the term. For a while, the young couple even went their separate ways, only to discover that being apart made them more miserable than being together. As time passed and the woman cried herself to sleep at night, and the man downed sleeping pills to get a night's rest, they both started to reevaluate the separation. Was what they were going through to be apart worth the agony? They both agreed that they once loved the other enough to commit their lives to a union, to parent children together."

Smiling, I reach for Melissa's

hand. Her skin is cold to the touch. "I might not know what day it is, and I can't recall my birth date, and I have no idea who the president of the United States is or the children in the various pictures hanging on the wall. But the one and only thing that *is* clear in my mind is that I know that love is only as solid as the man and woman's commitment. Grass is never greener on the other side; there's just more grass with the same stubborn weeds."

Sighing, I drop their hands and sit back, lost in vague reflections. The night that we reconciled, Jack and I climbed the stairs to the attic and located the star of Bethlehem Christmas ornament, and together we hung it on our mantle, a reminder of the most perfect love given to mankind, even if it was August in Vermont.

Silence lengthens. Finally Jack clears his throat. "You're speaking about you and Dad, aren't you? I didn't know you ever had trouble. I always thought the two of you had the perfect marriage."

"Me and Jack?" I burst out laughing. "There is no perfect anything, Jackie." The boyhood name slips out. "Jack can give as well as receive. Every marriage is slightly off-kilter, but you learn to deal with it." I pause and frown. "Was I talking about your father?"

His gaze slides to Melissa. "Mom, sometimes the stress builds. You do crazy things. . . .”

“Things you don’t mean. Maybe you misstate feelings when emotions run high,” Melissa adds. Their eyes meet and hold.

I sigh. “I often ask myself, ‘What is happiness, anyway?’ It’s just a word, and its value isn’t found in material things or in other people. It’s a state of mind, one never driven by circumstances. A person can search all his life only to discover the one thing he is looking for is patiently sitting on his doorstep.”

Jack Jr. shakes his head. “You’re remarkable. After everything you’ve been through and you can still find worth in life.”

“They say God looks after fools

and idiots." I grin. "I prefer the former."

When I see the couple out, an attendant rolls a cart down the corridor. A young man walks beside him. Jack Jr.'s eyes focus on the young woman who appears to be asleep. She puts me in mind of a young Melissa. Approximate age, small build, and dark hair. When Jack Jr. pauses to supportively shake the husband's hand (one of my Jack's traits), the man leans into him for the briefest of moments, clearly broken. I hear him say that a stroke has left his wife severely brain damaged and paralyzed. "She's thirty-three."

The shattered expression in my

son's eyes tells me that he recognizes that he's failed to acknowledge his abundant blessings.

In life, grass is only grass.

I don't know what's going on in Jack Jr. and Melissa's marriage. They may be happier than they've ever been or near the brink of despair, but if my being a mother has helped one tiny iota tonight, I couldn't or wouldn't ask for more.

The little blond girl who comes at Halloween is here again! The little cherub is growing up so fast that I barely recognize her. For some reason, she's here today, and she's not wearing a costume.

Her kisses and hugs are sweet and enthusiastic, and when I ask her age she holds up five fingers.

When Una stops by later, I try to explain how very much I miss my family. I think something bad has happened to Jack. The odd looks and abrupt change of subject when I mention his name leave me with stark fear that my love did not survive the accident. His absence leaves a crater in my heart so deep and endless that I know I'll never climb out. I tell myself that I must accept his absence, but my heart refuses the unspeakable loss.

Una has more wisdom than Solomon. She tells me, "You're a Christian, Arlene. You and your husband accepted the Lord at an early age. One day soon, you and Jack will be together. The brief time spent together on earth cannot compare with the eternal life you will spend together."

"If that's so, why doesn't someone tell me? Why do they leave me to guess about his absence?"

"Well, it's possible, dear," Una says in her wise way, "the doctors have warned that telling you everything about your prior life will only make matters worse."

This is the first thing Una has ever said that I find hard to believe. Right now, Jack is gone and each day it gets harder for me to hold on to hope.

My hand lifts to touch my temple. I'm not feeling well tonight. I sneeze twice during dinner, and the headache at the base of my neck throbs.

When I complain to the nurse, she says, "There's a bug going around. Stop by my cart before you go to bed. I'll give you something to make you sleep."

Sleep. That's all I get done here.

Chapter Thirteen

Fluffy, quarter-sized snowflakes drift outside from a murky sky. I sense a deep chill over the land as I sit in my armchair and watch white cotton balls fall from the sky. Darkness is coming. Tiny dancing lights illuminate the trees, and I wonder if angels are sitting above, having a delightful time creating the playful sight for my pleasure.

A nurse enters my room and chirps, "Are we ready to go?"

I turn to look at her. "Go where?"

She smiles, and I know what's coming next. "You're going to a party tonight." She bends close. "Remember? We've talked about it several times this week."

"We have?" I think she's mistaken. If someone had told me I was going to a party, I think I would remember.

The nurse straightens. "You have company tonight. Would you like to freshen up a bit?"

"What party?" I ask.

The nurse walks to my bed. "You've been a little down lately. Have you taken your afternoon meds?"

Like I have a choice? Someone sees that I down the horselike pills.

"You know, Arlene. The doctor

and your family want you to come out of your room and mingle more often." She sets a tray aside and punches the button so the head of the mattress lifts.

"I'm not sick?"

She pauses, her expression soft. "Why are you so unhappy, Arlene? I believe if you would participate more you would make a world of new friends and you wouldn't be so lonely."

I can't think of anything in particular that upsets me other than life.

"Well." She pats my hand gently. "I know your world has changed drastically, and I suppose anyone would feel a bit depressed."

Am I depressed? Is that why I

sleep so much?

"Come along, dear. Let's get you dressed. We don't want to keep —"

"Someone is coming to eat with me?" Expectancy swells. I've had very few eating guests since coming here. Una and I often share a sandwich at noon, but real company is a treat.

"What should I wear?"

The nurse steps to the closet and withdraws a pair of slacks and a green sweater. Frowning, I say, "The pants don't fit."

"They'll be fine. I love this sweater on you."

One look at the dark green garment and I know she's kidding. "You do? I don't recall wearing it."

"I believe your daughter-in-law

gave it to you last Christmas."

Which Christmas? The one before, before, before, or before that?

My eyes pivot to the pants. "Those, too?"

She nods, smiling. "Very pretty and festive ensemble."

My heart sinks. Chances are neither one would fit.

The sounds of happy chatter coming from the dining room meet me before my wheelchair turns the corridor corner. Surely something special is going on, but the nurse wheels me by the main entrance and pauses in front of a room — *the* room — the one where families come to eat.

"Here?" I ask, silently praying she

hasn't stopped to catch her breath.

"This is all for you tonight." Opening the double doors, she wheels me through. People rise to their feet, and I enter to a passionate round of applause. My eyes widen at the sight, and I focus on the festive, decorated tree sitting by the roaring fireplace. Centered in the top branch is the star of Bethlehem. The familiar sight brings hot tears to my eyelids.

"Mom!" Steven sets his glass aside and proceeds to welcome me. My bewildered gaze roams the room, and I am speechless when I focus on Jack Jr., Melissa, Steven, Julee, and little Ella.

Men are wearing tuxedos, and the women, long elegant gowns. I feel as though I've stepped straight back into my old life. Chair upon chair is occupied with people who I don't recognize. The special eating area is full to the brim!

"Steven, what is going on?"

"We're having family Christmas tonight, Mom."

"Christmas? It's Christmas again?" I swear the holiday rolls around faster than tax day.

Jack Jr. thanks the nurse and seizes my wheelchair. "Your party awaits, Milady."

Milady. The nickname bathes me in incredible sweetness. Someone very special once called me by that affectionate term.

Each strange face that I roll by brings a smile. Everyone in the room appears to know me, though I don't recognize one single guest other than my family. Jack Jr., Melissa, Steven, Julee — little Ella, who has my heart.

Hands reach out to touch me, to give me a tight squeeze. I must have many close friends and associates that I'm not aware of.

Jack Jr. seats me at the head of the long table, elegantly appointed with sparkling white china. I gaze at the long row of smiles and silently form the words on my lips. *Thank You, God.* For what, I'm not completely certain, but inside me I know that I, Arlene Santana, am receiving a special gift, one only God can provide.

Family, friends' warm smiles, and

happy tears.

I complain a lot to Una about this and that, but right now the only thought that runs through my mind is, *How blessed can one woman be?*

"Recognize the star, Mom?" Steven's voice breaks into my reflections.

"And the china," Melissa adds.

My gaze returns to place settings and then the tree, and I study the top ornament. The decoration seems out of place, and I can't say why. "Jack."

"You're right! It's yours and Dad's! Jack Jr. and I thought you might like to share it this Christmas."

Happiness like rich honey dribbles through my veins. "My,

my." That's all I can think to say. My china. My star of Bethlehem.

For this special moment, I am Arlene Santana, a woman whose world isn't turned upside down. Arlene living in a lovely home on the outskirts of Burlington, Vermont, with Jack, and a huge pine sitting in the den, east corner, our Christmas star shining into the dreariest night.

Hands reach out to touch me, to give me a squeeze. *Jack.* My eyes automatically search the crowd, but I know I won't find my husband's familiar grin. Gwendolyn lifts a hankie and waves. Eleanor snaps a picture, and Frances tries to catch my attention with a wolf whistle. I grin at my tablemates. We'll certainly have something to talk about tomorrow.

I am seated at the head of the long table, elegantly set with the finest china, my two sons and Ella close by. I gaze at the long row of smiles and silently thank God.

Family.

Friends.

I may have lost my memory, but the meaning of Christmas is intact and fully present in the room tonight.

Prime rib and baked potato is served. A large group of carolers wearing warm coats and bright scarves walk the hallways, singing carols of the season. Una and I have spent time trying to find places to hang our handmade ornaments and gifts that kind folks bring. I now have two new crocheted prayer shawls, more cookies than I can eat, and was that a children's group that brought watercolor-painted Christmas trees that now hang in my room?

Una!

I glance at Steven, who is sitting to my right. "Steven, where is Una?"

His fork pauses in midair, and a sheepish expression overtakes his features. He glances toward Jack Jr., who sits on my left side. "Jack?"

Melissa looks to Julee. "Oh Mom! Julee and I tried to invite her, but the nurses insist there isn't anyone here by that name. Is Una a nickname?"

I shake my head. "Why Una most certainly does live here." I don't know where some people get their ideas. Una, my best friend on earth, and they forget to invite her. The very idea that staff can mess up information and cause Una to miss my party. How do I explain the oversight to Una?

Julee glances at her diamond-encrusted wristwatch. "Do you think it's too late to invite her to join us? I'll be happy to get her. And explain the mix-up. What time is it?"

I purse my lips. Wake Una from a sound sleep and tell her she isn't invited to my party? I think not.

Jack Jr. consults his watch. "It's 8:10."

My heart plummets. The middle of the night. Lately, Una's in bed by seven thirty.

"I am so sorry, Mom." Melissa turns pleading eyes in my direction. It's hard to stay angry on such a near-perfect night. Making a resigned, throw-my-hands-up gesture, I continue with the meal, but the thought nags me. Una is missing all the fun.

"Really, Mom." Julee chews on her lip, clearly feeling concerned. "I wouldn't mind getting her and explaining."

"We can't bother her this late." By morning, I won't recall the party, so I guess Una's absence makes no difference. I just have to hope she isn't offended.

Toward the end of dinner, Chef rolls in a pastry cart and announces he will prepare bananas Foster for the guests.

"See? I remembered," Jack Jr. teases. "You and Dad never visited New Orleans without visiting Brennan's. This is your favorite dessert."

I don't recall, but the dessert looks fabulous.

After I scoop up every last drop of my treat, I push back and smile. "This is a most pleasant way to have fruit for the day."

Jolly laughter, a few presents, and then it is over. All beautiful things come to an end; I learned that the hard way.

Melissa approaches, beaming. "Guess what, Mom? The nurse

gave me permission to wake Una for a brief visit."

Jack Jr. frowns and checks the time. "It's almost ten o'clock. Do you think that's wise?"

Melissa's tone softens. "Honey, the nurse said she didn't think it would hurt this one time." She glances at me. "It will be much easier to explain the oversight now than later."

I can't contain my bubbly, almost childlike excitement. "I don't want to upset Una — but if she gets angry, she'll get over it. I make her mad all the time with some of my silly observations."

Waking her might not be the smartest solution, but Una's said a hundred times that she wants to meet my family, and better to tell her now about the mistake than in the morning when the party is over. I draw a deep breath.

I'm going for it.

The guests pull on coats and warm gloves, and Steven grabs hold of my wheelchair. "I'll walk Mom down the hallway." Fatigue overcomes me, but I have just enough strength for one very special Christmas visit.

"If you don't mind," a guest says. He has earlier introduced himself as Dale Miller, Jack's Air Force buddy. I have to take his word for the family connection. "Arlene, I'd like to meet your friend."

"Of course! Come along. Everyone come along!" I can picture me barging into Una's room in the dead of night, catching her in her flannel nightgown and mussed hair.

Before I know it, a line of guests trail us down the corridor, our festive mood catching. Nurses and aids pause to grin and with a finger to their lips gently hush the racket. Late nighters fill doorways wearing half-open robes and pajamas. Tired eyes focus on the merriment. Television sets blare from certain rooms. Surely Una will hear us coming.

Steven rolls me faster, apparently caught up in the celebratory mood. Others file in behind us, and I preen like a peacock with all the attention. "See my guests! We're on our way to meet Una," I call to fellow residents.

"Tell Una hi from me," a lady in pink sponge curlers calls.

The tip of Orville Myers's cane pokes through his half-open door. "Tell the ol' broad to come out of her room sometime."

I sniff and turn my head. The ol' diaper thrower is just plain cantankerous.

I feel a small hand grasp mine. Ella skips beside the wheelchair, pigtails bouncing. It seems that lately she stays longer. She often brushes my hair or rubs my stiff shoulder. We talk about me mostly. Her presence is like ointment on a nagging ache.

A woman's voice coaxes, "Ella, tell Grandma how much you

love her."

The little girl giggles and shakes her head negatively.

"Ella Parker," her mother chides.

My head whips around with the sound of the name. Ella Parker. I recognize that name. My grand-baby is Ella Parker. . . . The thought skips away.

The little cherub sticks her face through the handles of my wheel-chair. "I *love* you, Gramma." The statement is a little clipped but obe-dient.

Moisture fills my eyes, and I af-fectionately pat the little angel's shining hair. "Jack Jr. and Steven are here, too?" Can life be any bet-ter?

"We're all here, Mom." Whoever

acknowledges my question sounds very kind.

I suddenly hold up one hand as we near my room. "Steven, stop by my room first. Una might be asleep on my sofa. She often visits before she retires for the night."

"Whatever, Mom." Steven diverts the chair.

At my doorway, I call, "Una, are you in here? I'm bringing company!"

Sometimes Una doesn't look her best. She tries, and there isn't a vain bone in her body, but she likes advance notice before she meets strangers.

"Una, are you in here? I want you to meet . . ." I pause, turning to look at my handsome escort. "Jack Jr."

A blond head bends low. "Steven."

"Una?" I call. "She must be in the bathroom."

"We'll wait until she comes out." Steven pauses, but I shake my head. "She piddles a lot. I'm sure she's not . . . doing business. Roll me to the doorway."

When the wheelchair stops, I see that the bathroom door is wide open. "See. There she is."

Relief surges though my veins. It isn't often my family can spare time for my friends, and I can't miss this opportunity to introduce them.

Jack Jr. sends Melissa a questioning glance that makes me laugh.

"It's okay, Jack. Look." I nod for Steven to push me closer. When I enter the bathroom, I flip on the light and smile.

Peering inside the empty room, Jack Jr. frowns. "Where, Mom?" Others crowd in.

Pushing myself out of the chair, I grasp the security rail and jerk the string to my overhead light, and Una appears.

"There you are."

Steven and Jack Jr. crowd around me with Julee and Melissa on their heels. Everyone stares at the reflection in the bathroom mirror.

"Una dear," I say. "This is my family."

Chapter Fourteen

Just when I'm getting used to a season, a new one comes along. Patches of melting snow clutter the flower beds. The annual Christmas tree is gone. A few potted poinsettias with dropping leaves sit on fireplace mantles.

At night, the wind howls around the eaves of my corner room. Cozy fires blaze throughout the facility. During breakfast this morning, I saw a janitor tack up Easter bunnies in the hallway. Winter's grim shadows have given way to bright sunshine when I go to dinner tonight.

Una isn't the least bit upset about my family's late-night visit. She only laughs and says she welcomes family anytime they want to come, and she would have been plenty upset if I hadn't introduced her. No wonder. We had a marvelous visit, Una, me, my family, and friends.

Gwendolyn, Frances, and Eleanor say it's the best party they ever attended, and I am so blessed to have Steven and Jack Jr. for sons. I start to realize what they say is true. I've felt sorry for myself so long that I neglected to count the good things in life, things that matter. A warm bed. Friends. Food. I'm going to try harder to be happy.

My tablemates, who I often consider headaches, have become my "table" family. An occasional fuss erupts when Frances insists on poking or motioning instead of speaking when she wants something like salt, pepper, or butter. The woman does love her butter.

One night a server teases her and says her veins must look like L.A. five o'clock traffic. Frances gives him a stern look, suggestive of, "Take a close look, fella. Do I look like I worry about cholesterol at my age?" The young man stares back and then backtracks. He slides two fat chunks on the plate. "Here. Knock yourself out, kiddo."

Sniffing, Frances says, "Young

whippersnapper. I don't buy green bananas these days."

"Seen your family lately?" Gwendolyn taunts me and unfolds her napkin. She's in a feisty, almost carefree mood tonight. Even Frances, who barely cracks a smile, appears civil. Eleanor giggles twice. It seems like they're going somewhere — or plan to go. Maybe they've already gone. I can't keep up with their chatter.

I answer Gwen's question. "Jack Jr. was at my party."

"I know. I was there, too. Have you seen him lately?"

I sigh. "He calls, but I can't say when or how often."

Frances picks up a packet of jelly and studies it. "I hate that stuff they call 'jelly' they bring on our trays when we're sick. Tastes awful. Bland."

"What stuff is that, dear?" Eleanor pauses, her plate untouched.

"The jelly they bring on our breakfast trays when we have to eat in our room."

I can't recall any jelly that I've eaten that tastes bad, but then I rarely take meals in my room.

"Are you talking about the foil packet on your bedside table?" I venture.

"My bedside table? I thought it was on my tray. I like jelly, but that stuff would gag a maggot."

Gwendolyn glances at me and circles her temple with her forefinger before she addresses Frances.

"You're eating KY Jelly."

"That's what I said. What's with the jelly?"

"*Don't* eat that particular jelly. It's not for consumption."

"Then why do they bring it?"

I interrupt. "Eleanor, that's a lovely blouse you're wearing. I love blue." Eleanor doesn't have close family, only a nephew who lives out of state who occasionally brings her gifts.

"Thank you, lovey. It's a Christmas gift from Pete."

Frances is still mumbling, "Why would they bring you jelly if they didn't expect a body to eat it?"

I try to distract her. "You never married, Frances?"

"Never found Mr. Right. Contented myself with good books — literature mostly — music, working for the library, and donating any spare time to the Humane Society."

A scuffle breaks out near the nurse's cart. Loud voices fill the dining area: an irate man's overriding a woman's. "You tell that doctor that he is going to have to do *something* about these pills! They're *too* big to swallow. I have to cut them in half, and besides that, they gag me when I try to take them."

The elderly man slams the pills on the floor in front of the nurse and then stomps them, grinding the medication to mush with the heel of his boot.

The nurse's hand flies to her right

hip. "*Mr. Stern.* This rebellion is completely unnecessary. How many times must I remind you these are *suppositories*? You do *not* swallow them."

"I don't care what you call 'em. I'm *through* taking them!" He stalks off.

I turn back to my tablemates, used to the spectacles that take place on a daily basis. There's not a sane person in the building. "I've been thinking. Our families, or our savings, Steven informs me, allow us to be in the nicest of assisted-living facilities but it feels like living in a zoo. Do you agree?"

The three women nod in unison.

"Fruitcakes," Gwendolyn says. "Every last one except the staff, and there's a few of them that I'm starting to wonder about."

"Wackos," Frances allows.

Like eating KY Jelly is more sensible than consuming suppositories?

But I rarely permit myself to think of my real home. I don't know what's happened to the house; I only know I miss its welcome feel. Losing my mind is one thing, but losing my universe is another. I have been in here for years — maybe longer, and I accept that I will never again have the luxury of riding in my own car, or have the man at the local grocery cut a prime rib for Jack's and my dinner.

The acknowledgment saddens me as I wheel back to my room, where

I know Una is waiting. We'll chat, and then I will feel much better. She doesn't like it here, either. I'm still functional enough to believe that God is still in charge of my life, and there surely must be a reason why I live on. I have sons and family that don't forget me, unlike some here. Some live completely alone with only an occasional pastoral drop-in. I have phone calls and cards and pretty clothes that don't fit. I can't say that I'm neglected.

Admittedly if my family came every day, it wouldn't be enough. I have to make my own life, a woman advised me while we fashioned paper roses. I recall staring at the tissue paper wondering, *Why? Why do I have to make the best of nothing?* Why couldn't I have gone with Jack, and if not, why couldn't I be in my home, water my lovely tiger lilies, and feed the redbirds that flock outside my bedroom window, scrambling for seed in hanging feeders?

If I could go home, I would never make another tissue flower, or play another game of dominoes, and I'd most certainly stop squirrel counting.

I'd fill the days with warm sunshine, picnics, Caribbean cruises, and gelato. I'm not sure what gelato is, but I hear the nurses talking about the stuff. Salted pretzels. My mouth waters. Salt and pretzel. I'm pretty sure that I like both.

Instead, I am here in this big glass building with strangers — a sad, sad thought.

I am now a card-carrying member of the forgotten or discarded society.

When I enter my room, I'm surprised to see a nurse packing a large bag laid out on my bed. I stare at the strange sight and wonder if I've been kicked out. My heart races. Where will I go? When the nurse sees me, she hurriedly shuts the case. "Arlene! You're back from dinner early."

"Why are you packing that bag?"

"Why, for your trip tomorrow. Did you enjoy your meal? Smothered steak tonight, isn't it?"

"Meat loaf," I note absently.

"What trip? I'm not going anywhere." I try to recall if I've climbed over any counters to get Frances's mail — maybe I asked Candace one time too many for the name of her makeup foundation? Have I done anything or gone anywhere that I shouldn't? I come up blank.

Closing the double closet doors, the nurse smiles. "Arlene, we've talked about this often. You're going home tomorrow."

"But my family says this is my home."

And then it hits me. I am moving to another glass building. Exactly like this one but different.

I fumble with my blouse button, and the nurse helps me into my gown and then into bed. By the time I crawl between the sheets, I've forgotten the subject. I'm about to doze off when the door opens a crack and the same nurse appears, carrying a medicine cup. "Thought you might need a little something to make you sleep."

I had practically been asleep. "I don't think so. I'm pretty tired."

"Let's take it just the same." She pauses by the bedside with a small cup of water in her hand. I reach for the pill and obediently swallow it. Arguing does no good, and she might as well stop including herself in the process.

She never takes a pill in my presence.

■ ■ ■ ■

Early morning, I open my eyes to see the packed bag that's now sitting beside my door. What does that mean? Am I going somewhere?

"But what will Una think?" I complain when the nurse insists that I eat a light breakfast of toast and fruit. She then helps dress me warmly in slacks and a sweater. "I can't go anywhere without telling Una," I say, quite certain the staff is confused and has me mixed up with another patient.

"Honey, I was told to wake you at six, feed you a light breakfast, and have you dressed and waiting for your son and daughter-in-law."

"Are Steven and Julee coming?"

"I'm not sure; it might be your other son."

"I don't have another son. Steven is an only child."

"Okay, sweetie." Her eyes make a final sweep of the room. "I believe you're ready to go."

"I'm not going anywhere without Una."

Una appears to be forgotten in the big rush. I have no more sat down in my wingback chair to await something than Steven and Julee show up, all smiles.

"Morning, Mom." Steven gives me an absent peck, his eyes sweeping the room. "Everything packed and ready to go?"

"She's a bit confused this morning," the nurse says. "She doesn't recall you telling her about the move."

"Okay." He flashes me a smile. "Everything's cool, Mom. You're in good hands." He nods to the nurse. "Thank you. You and the entire staff have been very kind to her. You have our deepest gratitude."

The woman smiles and reaches for my hand. "She's easy to be kind to. We will miss you, Arlene."

Crossing my arms, I remain seated. "I'm not going anywhere."

"Bring the wheelchair," Steven says.

Before I can say *diddly spit,* I am in my wheelchair rolling down the hallway. When we approach the entrance, Dr. Important glances up. "Good morning, Arlene. We're going to miss you."

My jaw drops. The man has never said a word to me. I find my manners. "Thank you, Dr. Important."

He smiles. "The name's Cliff."

"Cliff." I turn in my wheelchair to stare at him as Stephen pushes me out the door of the big building with all the shiny glass and helps me into the backseat of his pickup truck. Still cross armed, I try everything to prevent my son from buckling me in, but my actions prove futile. I hear a snap, a door shut, and then Steven appears in the driver's seat, adjusting the rearview mirror. Julee's already seated.

"I'm not going anywhere," I call — in case they miss the hint.

Manicured lawns with patches of

dirty snow clutter the gardens as the vehicle rolls along the winding driveway. Despite my protests, it does appear that I am leaving. "Una," I whisper, pressing my hand to the cold glass. Tears swell to my eyes. How can I leave Una? Life is barely tolerable now; how can this man and woman take me away from the only thing that I know?

How will Jack find me?

"Listen, I really can't go, but thank you anyway." A more horrified thought comes to mind. "The little girl that you bring to see me — she won't know where to find me. I am very fond of her, Steven. I don't want to leave — I'll never see her again!"

"Ella will find you, Mom. Julee

and I will bring her often."

"It's okay." Julee turns to hold my hand. "Everything is fine. Don't worry. We promise to take good care of you. There's nothing to be concerned about or afraid of."

I grasp her hand and then drop it. "I want to go home."

"You are going home. Very soon now you'll be where you're happy." She glances at Steven, and I guess they think I'm deaf, too. "She doesn't recall anything that the doctors or we have told her about the move."

"She'll be fine once she gets there."

"I don't want to go to another building," I clarify. "Take me to *my* home."

The long drive worries me; automobiles and semitrailer trucks clog the highway. By now I cease to talk or argue. It seems I have no choice in this matter.

Eventually the vehicle turns off, and I close my eyes, sensing I must be very close to wherever I am going. Through slatted eyelids, I watch as we approach a small brick building. I drop my hands, and my eyes fasten on the plane that sits in front of the terminal. My stomach lurches. Something about the plane upsets me. I make out the name, written in bold red lettering: SANTANA TOYS. Then in smaller letters are the words FAMILY OWNED AND OPERATED.

"I don't like planes," I say.

Steven says, "You love to fly, Mom."

Now they're telling me my likes and dislikes. Isn't there anything that is mine alone?

Julee reaches back to pat my hand. "Relax. Everything is going to be fine."

Fine? I've forgotten the definition of the word, but I reason that *fine* doesn't fit my circumstance.

"Jack," I call. He can't hear me, but his name makes me feel more secure.

Setting the brake, Steven steps out of the truck, and I see Jack Jr. walking out of the terminal. I draw in a quick breath, intensely conscious of how father and son favor each other. The brothers shake hands and exchange words.

A van pulls up beside us, and I note the name written on the side: SUNSET GARDENS OF BUCKHEAD. Inside the bus, three gray-headed old ladies wearing hats turn to crane their necks toward the pickup.

Julee slides out and reaches for the backdoor handle. I think this is my cue to exit, but I hesitate. My mind is spinning. Nothing I'm witnessing makes sense. Opening the door, my daughter-in-law eases me out, and I hear voices talking — Jack Jr. and a man whom I don't recognize.

"Morning, Jack! You behind the controls this morning?"

"Never miss an opportunity to fly.

How's the wife, Skip?"

"Doing well. Her mother lives with us now. Keeps life interesting."

Before I can say *Jack Sprat,* Steven and Jack Jr. load me into the plane and then take my bag from Melissa. Cupping my elbow, Melissa seats me up front, and my jaw drops when I see someone has loaded my tablemates.

Gwendolyn, Frances, and Eleanor grin. "Are you surprised?" they chirp in unison.

Surprised? I couldn't be more startled if I woke up with a rattlesnake in my pajamas. I'm certain that I look like I've been caught in headlights.

Once I'm strapped in, Steven

steps into the plane and kneels before my seat. He gently takes my hand. "Mom, I know you're confused, but the doctors, Jack Jr. and I, Missy and Julee — we have told you about this move. You agreed. You're going home, Mom."

"Home?" I shake my head, near tears from the strange excursion. "I don't know where that is, son."

"It's a very happy place in Vermont with big rooms, and all of Dad's things are there as he left them. Jack Jr. and I closed the house after the accident. We haven't known what to do with it, but the answer came the night of your Christmas party. With the help of more cleaners, lawyers, and paperwork than you can imagine; endless family conversations with Frances's, Eleanor's, and Gwendolyn's kin and guardians; more papers, more lawyers, hiring a full-time nurse and small staff; the old home place is back in fine shape. Seems Jack Jr. and I have opened a new business."

"Is Jack there?"

My son's eyes soften to liquid love. "In so many ways, Mom, he's there. Not physically, but his big chair is there, the bed you shared is there, his razor, his coffee mug. When you're ready, we'll store his things. But for now, I want you home, to look out the big windows and watch your birds in their feeders, your lovely tiger lily flower garden. You'll get to see them bloom this summer. Dad's there, and you should be with him."

Frances blows her nose harshly and then states, "We get to live with you until we croak."

At the moment, Steven's words fail to register. My Jack is gone, but considering how very much I miss him, I can allow my son to dream, can't I? And the word *home*? I mentally try the word on and find it fits perfectly, like rainbows and summer showers.

Steven grins. "We thought it appropriate that our first guests to occupy 'Arlene's Place' should be your tablemates."

Frances sticks the hankie in her purse.

My son continues. "Like I said,

you'll have all the help you need, and Ella will be underfoot a lot. Julee and I are going to relocate — move back to Vermont. We plan to run Arlene's Place, and my foreman will run the electrical business here in Atlanta. All you girls need to do is put on a couple of Elvis CDs, roll your hair in orange juice cans, and parrrteee."

"Steven," I admonish. "I may be nuttier than a rabid bulldog, but even I know women do not roll their hair in orange juice cans any longer." Well, there is one woman in the complex that still does, but she's got to be the exception. "What about Una?" They've neglected to include her again.

Steven's tone drops. "Una can't

come, Mom. Jack Jr. and I don't think that's wise. If, after you settle in, you still feel that you need her, we'll arrange something."

I slowly lift my eyes to meet his. "Promise?"

He squeezes my hand. "You got my word."

I hear last-minute groundwork under way outside of the plane. Melissa had seated me next to Gwendolyn, and she now checks my belt. "Too tight?" she asks.

"Just fine — everything is fine now."

"This is cool," Gwendolyn says. "We're roomies."

I really wish I recalled that particular conversation — but friends are good.

"I'm scared of these death traps." Frances shifts in her seat, rechecking her seat belt.

"Please refrain from calling the plane a 'death trap' while we're in flight." Eleanor snaps her belt closed. "Has my lipstick worn off?" She fumbles for her purse.

"You're not afraid of flying, dear. You're afraid of crashing." Gwendolyn slips a piece of gum in her mouth. "Here, this prevents you from going deaf during the flight."

"Not deaf," I correct. "Chewing gum helps to clear your ears."

"Of what?" Gwen asks.

"Never mind."

Jack Jr. calls from the pilot's seat. "Ready to go, ladies?"

Melissa moves back and heaves

the door closed and locks it. She gives me a little squeeze as she walks to her husband, bends to give him a tender kiss, and then takes the copilot's chair. The touching exchange makes me cry harder — and laugh at the same time.

Here I was, thinking that God might be neglecting me.

And then the private jet is screaming down the runway, and suddenly I feel liftoff. Lighter than air, a mere bubble dancing through clouds, I soar up . . . up toward the heavens.

The plane climbs through layers of fluffy clouds, bright, intense splashes of blue, and I imagine that I see angels waving to me. Gwendolyn's leather seat and mine face the cockpit, and I can see every movement. The air is as smooth as melting ice cream. The craft gently levels off, and my journey home begins.

The pilot turns slightly in his seat and asks, "Are the ladies comfortable?"

Voices speak up. "Great!"

"I'm going to be sick. This thing got barf bags?"

I hear the distinct sound of retracting landing gear then a lipstick cap being replaced. "This sucker can go, can't she?"

And then the pilot focuses on me, and a veil drops away and I am looking into my Jack's eyes, eyes that I have adored for most of my adult life, the eyes of love. "And you, Milady?"

Milady. A slow, probably slightly naughty smile spreads across my face, and I can't stop grinning. My gaze locks with his, and I nod. "I'm perfect, Jack. Now."

"Good." He winks. "Let's go home."

ABOUT THE AUTHOR

Lori Copeland is a popular best-selling author of both historical and contemporary fiction. Her books have been nominated for the prestigious Christy Award, and she received two *Romantic Times* Lifetime Achievement Awards. Lori makes her home in Missouri with her husband, Lance, three sons, and ever growing family. Her hobby is knitting prayer and friendship shawls and baking chocolate chip cookies.

The employees of Thorndike Press hope you have enjoyed this Large Print book. All our Thorndike, Wheeler, and Kennebec Large Print titles are designed for easy reading, and all our books are made to last. Other Thorndike Press Large Print books are available at your library, through selected bookstores, or directly from us.

For information about titles, please call:
(800) 223-1244

or visit our Web site at:
http://gale.cengage.com/thorndike

To share your comments, please write:
Publisher
Thorndike Press
10 Water St., Suite 310
Waterville, ME 04901